1

fetish play. This e-book is for sale to adults ONLY, as defined by the laws of the country in which you made your purchase. Please do not try any new sexual practice, especially those that might be found in our BDSM/ Fetish titles without the guidance of an experienced practitioner. Neither Bitten Press, nor its authors, will be responsible for any loss, harm, injury or death resulting from use of the information contained in any of its titles.

Publisher's Note: This is a work of fiction. All characters, places, businesses, and incidents are from the author's imagination. Any resemblance to actual places, people, or events is purely coincidental. Any trademarks mentioned herein are not authorized by the trademark owners and do not in any way mean the work is sponsored by or associated with the trademark owners. Any trademarks used are specifically in a descriptive capacity. Final edits rest with the author of this work.

Bitten Press: Thank you for purchasing this title. We support authors and ask you to remember that the only money most authors make from writing comes from book sales. If you like this work, please check for upcoming titles from this author via the link on our website and spread the word. If you see "free shares" offered or cut-rate sales on pirate sites, please report the offending entry to the editor Bitten Press. Thank you for not pirating our titles.

Other Books by AJ Storm

Emily's Passion:

Review:

Finallv
By Kindle Customer on August 22, 2015
Format: Kindle Edition Verified Purchase
Being a woman in her late 50s and having a long distance D/s on line relationship, that will be in RL in a couple of years, I questioned my sanity. My kids pretty much have me buried in a pine box because a woman My age should not have desires. I should be content bring a grandmother and help raise my grand kids. I shouldn't want to dress sensuous and feel sexy. My Dom makes me feel like Emily in this book. This book helped me feel more confident in my choice of life style . Made me feel " I am not dead, I still have life in me and by God I plan to enjoy it". Ty A J Storm for writing about us older women who are like a fine wine.

DARK STRANGERS

Alexanders' Story

The Power of Two

Fortune's Eyes

Acknowledgement The author acknowledges the trademarked status and trademark owners of the following word-marks mentioned in this work of fiction.

Six Flags over New Orleans

Dodge Challenger

Cherry Picker

Wiccan

Celtic

Cajun

Café Du Monde

Voodoo/Hoodoo

Tarot Cards

Jax Burger

Jackson Brewery Bistro Bar

Shibari

Ferris Wheel

Bordeaux

Woldonberg Park

Doobie Brother's – The Doobie Bros. Corporation

Jump (For My Love) – Gary Paul Skardina, Marti Sharron, Sony/ATV Tunes LLC, Anidraks

Music, Emi April Music Inc., Stephen Mitchell Music, Warner-tamerlane Publishing

Corporation

The Pointer Sisters – The Partnership Pointer, The Pointer Sisters

Jumpin Jack Flash – Jagger/Richards, Bill Wyman, Abkco Music, Inc.

Dedication

Thank you to my friends and co-workers at Bitten Press LLC for their support, encouragement, and friendship. You forced me out of my comfort zone, and though I fought you, you made me strong. I appreciate the love of my author friends and you know who you are.

It goes without saying, I always love and appreciate the support, encouragement, opinions, and suggestions from my faithful beta reader, Jody Rhoton. You are always such a blessing. Two more readers I would like to mention are

Tina England and Teresa (SWEET T) Adams. Ladies, your unbiased opinions on my finished work gave me incredible strength. Hugs to you.

Sara Davis, you turned into the greatest right hand that I have ever had. Whatever I've asked you to do, you've done and gone even further. Thank you for your help, love, and support. You're are officially dubbed The Bomb PA.

I have many friends who constantly encourage me to write. There's no way possible to name each one but your friendship and loyalty mean the world to me. Thank you so very much.

My husband is my biggest fan and this book definitely made an impression on him. I hope his "gut feelings" are right. Last fall, I took a trip to New Orleans and fell in love with the city. I knew I had to write a fictional romance based in that wonderful and exciting place. One day I will take him back to NOLA with me. Thanks go out to my hubs for letting me read every word out loud to him and listen to his suggestions. And of course, I always thank him for putting up with my craziness when I'm writing.

Last but not least, I want to thank those who take the time to buy and read my work. The readers are the most important audience and fan base an author can have. You have my heart and my loyalty.

Fortune's Eyes
Prologue

The young woman stood on the balcony, looking down at the street below. People from various backgrounds roamed the thoroughfare, even at this ungodly hour. Smells from the French Quarter assaulted her nose with all ethnicities of food and alcohol mixed with urine, vomit, stagnant rain water, and yes, even sex. She gripped the railing of the balcony as clouds of memories transported her back in time.

A small wisp of a child cowered between the refrigerator and the wall of a tiny kitchen. He towered over the child pointing his finger at her face. The man was tall with a massive chest, which at one time could have been considered ripped. Handsome, but not a lady killer, his dark hair was thinning and greying at the temples. His voice bellowed through the small room as he moved closer to the trembling child.

"Adaleena, you come out of that corner now. I want an explanation for the lies you told at school." The little raven haired girl crept from her hiding place and sat at the feet of her father. Tears streamed down her face as she looked up into his piercing eyes.

"Papa, I didn't lie. I saw it when Billy Ray grabbed my arms before he pushed me down. I told him what I saw. He laughed at me, but I could tell by his eyes he was afraid of me."

"You're never to tell your wild tales again, young lady. You hear me?"

"I didn't tell tales, Papa. Why don't you believe me?"

A raised hand swinging toward her face was the last thing she saw as a male voice hollering from the street below drew her from her memories.

"Hey beautiful, how much for an hour?"

She looked at the drunk man weaving where he stood.

Not very likely he could find the right place, let alone put it in.

"Go away, dreamer. I'm not a whore."

She heard him yell 'Bitch' as she moved through the French doors back into her apartment. A silver-haired, round woman was hanging Adaleena's clothes in the closet. The woman was dressed in colorful Boho clothing, which only enhanced the warm smile reaching all the way to her eyes including a twinkle. Rings and bracelets were creating their own melody as the woman moved her hands, placing the girl's clothing on hangers.

"Hush, Leena, some of my close friends make their living bringing a bit of happiness to the men who seek a night of love."

"How can you call it love, Nana, when it's just sex for hire?"

Even though the woman was her aunt, she'd always called her Nana. She'd been the only one who'd believed Leena's stories, and the only one who'd ever shown her tenderness. Her aunt had moved away when the girl was ten, causing her to feel abandoned.

"Nana, why did you move away and leave me?"

"When your mother died, your father didn't want me around any longer. He called me a Bohemian and said I was a bad influence. Because I believed your stories and encouraged you to listen to them, he accused me of trying to turn you away from him. Your gift is special, my darling, and you shouldn't be shunned the way his congregation shunned anyone who didn't fit their mold."

"You could have taken me with you?"

"No child, you know your father never would have allowed it. He and his cronies would've come after both of us and I'd have been thrown in jail for kidnapping. As far as your father was concerned, if I stayed I would've never been allowed to see or talk with you again. So I left knowing I could contact you as much as I wanted."

"He constantly told me I was evil and going to hell. 'God will never hear your cries because what you see is straight from Satan himself' is what he told me every day. When I turned fourteen, I refused to step into his church again. For some strange reason, he never fought me about it. I guess his congregation convinced him I didn't belong."

"Honey, my brother was a very bitter man raised by an overbearing, stern father. He forced your father into the

AJ Storm

ministry and crammed hell and damnation down his throat. Not that I'm making excuses for how he treated you and your mother. It just wasn't right."

"How on earth did you turn out normal?"

She watched as her aunt rolled her head back and gave a loud belly laugh, warming the mood with pure love and joy.

"Very few people would call me normal, Leena. I'm a free spirit with gifts of laughter, honesty, wisdom, joy, and love to share with those who need them."

Wrapping her arms around the silver-haired woman, she hugged her tight, craving the warmth only her Nana could give.

"Okay, young lady, it's late. We should at least try to get a few hours' sleep. I'm so glad you came, and I'm right next door if you need anything. Sweet dreams, baby."

"Goodnight Nana and thank you. I love you."

Her body was tired, and rather than wash up before climbing into bed, she simply stripped down to her panties and slid between the sheets. The bed felt good, molding to her body as she snuggled under the thick covers. She was safe, but most of all, this was a place where she definitely was loved. Sleep consumed her, and for once her dreams were peaceful.

****

The sun peeked through a gap in the curtains, landing directly in Leena's eyes. She groaned, throwing a pillow over her face and snuggled further under the covers. A delicious smell of cooked bacon drifted under the pillow, teasing her nose. Her stomach growled and she realized she'd never go back to sleep.

The covers were thrown back and her toes stretched all the way to the end of the bed. Her body tightened as she extended her muscles to their limit.

God, that feels good.

Sliding off the bed, she made her way to the bathroom and took care of business. Thankfully, she had hot water when she turned on the shower and stepped under the spray. She let the water run down her head, through her long dark curls, and onto her body. Her stomach growled again so she hurried to wash and towel off.

Water dripped from her hair onto her shoulders, so she toweled the excess off the curls. Rather than dry her hair with a blow dryer, she fluffed and scrunched it with her fingers. There was enough natural body in it allowing the hair to have a slight curl when air dried.

Her aunt kept a full length mirror hanging on the outside of the bathroom door. She stood in front of the mirror staring at her dark beige skin. It was smooth and looked as if she had a constant tan. Her father's side of the family were Italian and she had all the characteristics of his genes. However, her mother's family were gypsies, which only added to her coloring. She often wondered what drew her father to marry her mother. They were nothing alike.

Focused on her face, her eyes then dropped to the rest of her body. She frowned…she took after her aunt. Ample curves tapered into a slender waist but she only saw her hips and thighs.

Refusing to look any longer, she threw on a tight pair of jeans and t-shirt, stepping out into a hallway. Her aunt owned the building they were in. She'd inherited it from her husband who'd passed on five years ago. The bottom floor consisted of her business and the top was the living quarters. It was a large four room apartment with two bedrooms which shared a huge bathroom. The kitchen/dining and living rooms were separated from the bedrooms by a hallway straight through the middle.

"Nana, I smell coffee and bacon. Tell me you made scrambled eggs and biscuits with them."

When she strolled into the kitchen, her aunt was standing over the stove. The small dining table sat in a small breakfast nook with three windows looking out over the street. It was set for two with orange juice poured into small glasses.

"I sure did, baby. You know I believe in a good, healthy breakfast to start the day. Sit yourself down and start on your juice. The biscuits are almost ready to come out of the oven."

Leena sat at the table and sipped her juice. She gazed out the window, amazed people were out and about this early in the morning. "Don't people ever sleep around here? They were out on the street when I went to bed and they're there this morning."

"The French Quarter is always busy…between the regulars and the tourists, it stays this way." Dishing the eggs onto Leena's plate, she watched her aunt turn and retrieve the biscuits from the oven. "Butter these up while they're good and hot. They'll melt in your mouth."

"God, it smells so good. Is the coffee ready?"

"Yes, child. Did you drink all your juice?"

"Yes, I did, Nana."

The old woman poured her niece a large cup of coffee and sat down in the chair across from her. "So, are you here for a visit or are you planning on staying?"

Her mouth was full, having devoured her biscuit in two bites. She waited until she swallowed before she answered. "I was hoping you'd let me stay. I'm not sure exactly what I'll do to make money, but I won't freeload off you, Nana. I simply want to be with you."

"Exactly what I wanted to hear, child. You don't have to contribute money to me. I'm doing just fine and I want you to stay here with me. If you absolutely have to keep yourself busy, I can help find something at one of my friends' shops. But you know, I can use some help in my shop. I can't pay much, but it'll keep you busy if it's what you're after. You'd be perfect."

"Whatever you need…I'm your girl. I've worked retail, bartended, car hopped…you name it, I've done it."

"Oh and before I forget, I'm closing the shop early this evening. Several of my friends who also tell fortunes are having a meeting along with dinner. I imagine it will be a very late night, so don't worry and don't wait up for me. This afternoon, I'll show you the shop and the parlor at the back. You'll probably meet several of my regulars and friends who'll drop in for a bit. I strive for a relaxed atmosphere in my shop…a friendly one. It promotes great business, plus lets me in on all the local gossip." She winked at her niece.

"Okay, Lady, I promise I won't send the troops out after you. I'm sure you're a smart girl and can get out of any trouble you happen to cause."

"Oh, we don't cause trouble, child…we create it." She paused for a moment and then continued.

"How's your card skills? Have you kept practicing what I taught you when you were little, or did your father put a stop to that as well?"

"Yes, I kept practicing. I hid it from him while I lived at home. Once I was on my own, I was able to do more and study them. I'm not bad but not as good as you."

"Pfft, I'll have you reading like an expert before you can say psychic. Hey, do you still do that thing with your eyes?"

Leena burst out laughing shaking her head. "Nana, I never did anything with my eyes. They naturally change colors when the mood is right. Daddy always accused me of being a witch because of them."

"What do you mean when the mood is right? One minute they would be a beautiful light hazel color and the next, they were a brilliant green. I could swear they almost glowed at times."

"Okay, now you're simply exaggerating."

"Well, it looked as if they did. I never would've thought a dark haired beauty such as you, would ever have such green eyes. You don't see it very often. Why are you frowning at me?"

"Because I'm not a beauty…never have been."

"Baby girl, you listen to me right now. You put all of those things your father told you right out of your head. The man was pure meanness and he would've told a beauty queen, her body was fat and ugly. He lied to you, child, and don't you forget it. You're beautiful and always were."

She smiled at her aunt, grateful she'd come to see her. She'd missed the warmth and love this lady always gave to her.

"Now, let's go downstairs and see what kind of trouble we can get into."

"I'll be down in a minute, Nana. Just need to hit the bathroom once more."

Chapter One

Leena awoke to pounding on the door to the outside stairwell. She crawled out of bed throwing on an old football jersey which barely covered her ass.

"Dammit, Nana. I knew you'd forget your keys," she mumbled shuffling toward the door.

Unlatching the three chain locks, she then unlocked the two deadbolts and finally threw the door open to excruciatingly bright sunshine. She expected to see her Nana. Since the sun was directly overhead, she knew it had to be almost noon.

Two men stood at the top of the stairs holding their badges in front of her eyes, where she could see them. The tall dark-brown haired detective spoke. "I'm detective Roger Black and this is detective Bryan Hall. We're with the New Orleans homicide division. Does Addie Price live here?"

She stared harder at their credentials, comparing their pictures to their faces. Fear threaded its way through her mind.

"Yes, she does. Why do you ask?"

"And you are?" Roger asked closing his billfold.

Her body buzzed with panic. She took a step back and leaned against the doorjamb for support.

"Addie's my aunt. I'm Leena. Why are you asking me this? What's happened?"

"Is there somewhere we can talk, please?" Bryan asked.

She barely heard his question as her mind became numb.

"Miss?" Roger interrupted.

"Uh, I'm sorry…yes…please, come in." On auto-pilot, she moved out of the way and allowed them to enter the apartment. Leading them down the hall to the living room, her hand motioned toward the couch while she sat in a chair across from them.

"What's this about, Detective?"

Roger answered. "I'm afraid we have bad news, Leena. Your aunt's body was found early this morning in an abandoned warehouse. Her body was tied to a St. Andrew's cross. I'm sorry to have to tell you, she was stabbed multiple times and bled to death."

Leena felt sick to her stomach. Silent tears streamed down her face, while she searched theirs for any hope of a mistaken identity.

"No, you're wrong. She left last night for dinner with friends and came home late. I bet she's asleep in her bed right now." She stood up intending to make her way to her aunt's bedroom and see for herself. Detective Hall gently held her shoulders preventing her from leaving the room.

"Miss, you won't find her there. Her purse was found near the body with her identification in it. Apparently, it wasn't a robbery because it still had her credit cards and money in it. Please, sit down before your knees give out from under you."

She fell back into the chair resting her head on the back cushion. Bryan raced into the kitchen pulling drawers and cabinet doors open, until he found what he wanted. He came back into the living room with a wet cloth. Before he could hand it to her, the color leeched out of her face and she leaned over throwing up in her lap and all over her feet. This went on for approximately three minutes and when her body finally stopped heaving, she took the cloth wiping her mouth. It was at this time she remembered she only had on a short football jersey and nothing else.

"Shit. I've made a mess."

Roger jumped up and ran into the kitchen grabbing every towel he could find. He drenched them all and proceeded to mop the floor around her feet. On his knees, she noticed his head was level with her knees, and quickly pulled them together.

"I'm a mess...I need a shower. I can't stay like this."

Bryan helped her step over the mess on the floor. "You get cleaned up and we'll have this mopped up when you're through. We have a few questions, so we'll still be here."

Leena staggered into her room, closed the door, and slid to the floor. Her body trembled fighting back sobs and anger.

I need to keep control.

Pushing herself off the floor, she moved into the bathroom and turned the water on in the shower. She removed her jersey and wadded it up tossing it in the trash can. Hot water pelted her shoulders, sending a cloud of steam rising into the air. Heat building in the shower consumed her body and mind. Thoughts of her childhood drifted her mind back in time...she always was told she caused trouble. In her mind, this situation was no different than the past. If she'd simply stayed away from her aunt, she'd still be alive.

Her hands fisted, pounding the tiles on the wall over and over releasing her rage. The more she pounded, the more her whimpers turned into sobbing and then into screams. When her spirit accepted her Nana was truly gone, she raised her eyes to the ceiling and shrieked curses at God.

How could He take away the one person who truly loved me?

She collapsed against the wall, sliding down to the tile floor. A crumpled pile of naked flesh, her body automatically curled into a fetal position. She remained there even when the hot water became cold.

A knock on the bathroom door barely roused her from her mourning. She chose to ignore the detective's calling. The door was thrown open, and she vaguely was aware Roger reached in turning off the water. He grabbed the towels hanging on the bath bar and wrapped her body with them. Then he lifted her off the floor carrying her to her bed.

"I'm sorry, Leena. This was too much for you. We can wait to ask our questions tomorrow after you've slept. Is there someone who we can call for you to stay here tonight?"

"Um…no. Nana was the only one here in town I knew. I'll be all right. I need to sleep."

His touch was gentle as he tucked her under the covers. He pulled a chair over near the head of the bed and sat in it. She watched him until she could no longer keep her eyes open.

****

Roger leaned against the back of the chair observing the young beauty as she fell asleep. He worried about her state of mind and wondered if they'd handled it wrong. Especially, after her episode in the shower. They'd followed proper protocol but maybe they could've been less professional and more compassionate. Her screams had brought him running into her room and he'd found her on the shower floor in the fetal position, whimpering.

Bryan left, promising to return with breakfast the next morning. Roger watched the rise and fall of her breathing, unable to not think back to when he found her on the shower floor.

He knew he shouldn't stare at her body, but God, she was beautiful. Long, dark hair hung in wet curls down her back and across her shoulders. Her skin was golden, smooth and supple, begging for his lips to taste and nibble. God help him, he tried so hard not to look at her breasts but when he picked her up, they stood firm in front of his eyes. His cock responded to the visual display, strongly pressing against the fly of his pants. Then he saw them. Perky and pink, her nipples stood erect...ripe for the taking.

Sweat poured down his neck, but told himself it was the shower, even though the heat had been dissipated long ago. Gaining control of himself, he quickly wrapped her in towels and placed her in her bed, drawing the covers above her breasts.

A soft voice roused him from the deep sleep he'd fallen into. He didn't know whether to be thankful or not being awakened from his erotic memories.

"Roger?"

"Roger, you awake?"

"I am now." He woke groggy and sat up slowly in the chair. "How are you, darlin? Did you sleep any?"

"A little, not much."

"Bryan's bringing breakfast in a bit. Nothing fancy, just bacon and cheese croissants. I'll put on a pot of coffee if you have any."

"I do, but before you do, I've got to ask you how Nana died."

"Leena, I don't think you're ready for the answer. Maybe we should wait until the hurt is not so strong."

"No, I want to know now. My emotions are under control. Please, tell me what happened."

He sat up straight with clenched hands on his knees. This usually wasn't a problem for him but this woman was different. She'd touched some place deep in his heart and the thought of breaking hers upset him.

"Okay, but I want you to know up front if you get sick again or start crying out of control, I will stop. You understand?"

"Yes. I'm okay with it."

"The night security guard found her early this morning, when his shift ended. Her body was tied to a portable Saint Andrews cross and left there. Cause of death appears to be exsanguination. We'll know more after the autopsy later today. There was a single deep cut across her right jugular vein. She also had deep gashes across the inside of each wrist. They appeared to be precise in width and depth."

"Dear God." She'd covered most of her body with the sheet and he watched her wrap her arms around her middle rocking back and forth.

"Are you all right to go on? It's not all of the facts."

"I'm okay. Keep going."

"There's one really strange fact...no blood was found at the crime scene except what was left on the dagger. It was lying in front of the cross at her feet. No prints were on the dagger...just your aunt's blood."

"How can that happen? I don't understand."

"Neither do we, Leena. No prints were found anywhere in the warehouse and her purse hadn't been touched. We finger printed it and only found your aunt's. We're stumped. There's absolutely no leads at the moment."

Bryan came into the room carrying a box of croissants.

"Good morning. I'm guessing you told her about the crime scene?"

"Yes, she asked and as long as she handled it, I thought she had a right to know all the facts."

She gazed over at him and he thought she looked like a little girl lost. He wanted to drape himself around her and keep out all the bad vibes.

Not appropriate, Roger. Pull your head out, man.

"All right, let's take a break and eat. Do we have any coffee made?" Bryan asked.

"Sorry, man, I fell asleep and didn't wake up. I'll make some now."

Roger stood and turned toward the door with his fellow detective following. He closed the door behind them allowing her the privacy to get dressed.

Bryan sat at the table while Roger made coffee. "How do you think she really handled it?"

"I think she's in shock, Bry. I really don't think it's actually hit her yet but she at least didn't fall apart today. Have you heard anything else this morning?"

Bryan answered, "Only the official COD was exsanguination and the dagger was used as the weapon. Nothing we didn't already know. It also appears something was inserted into the jugular by the way the skin was stretched but nothing was left behind."

She came out of her room and both men stopped talking at once. Taking the chair across from Bryan, she sat as Roger poured the coffee.

"I'm really fine, guys. You don't have to tiptoe around me."

After filling their cups with coffee, he searched the cabinets and found small plates. Tongs hung over the stove and he used them to place a croissant on each plate. After he passed the plates out, he sat down in between the two.

Both men watched her take a bite of the pastry and sighed a sigh of relief.

Roger was nervous and cleared his throat several times. Finally he asked, "Do you know if your Aunt was into BDSM?"

Taking a sip of her coffee, she choked and he felt he had to keep explaining. "You know what BDSM is? Sexual kink, dominants and submissives? Shit, I'm not doing a very good job of this."

"I know what BDSM is. I simply don't understand why you'd ask if my aunt participated in it."

"I was simply trying to establish a relationship between the victim and the cross she was tied to."

"Victim? You act like she didn't have a life or a name. Her name was Addie…Addie Price. And no, she wasn't into BDSM."

He took a drink of his coffee, looking to Bryan for help. "I had to ask, Leena. I'm sorry if I offended you."

"I want to see the crime scene."

"It's impossible. You aren't part of the investigating team," interrupted Bryan.

"The hell I'm not. She was my family and I'm going to find out who and why? If you won't help me, I'll do it myself."

He stared at Roger and then back to her. Roger spoke up. "Officially, I can't allow it. I can force the situation and process an order to prevent you from being within fifty feet of the scene."

She slammed her cup on the table and pushed her chair back. Her anger filled the room.

"Now wait a minute…I said officially. Unofficially, I want you safe and out of harm's way. I'll take you there if you promise not to go all tough guy on me. We'll go once they finish processing everything."

When he saw her body relax, he silently sighed a thank you knowing he'd gotten through to her.

Chapter Two

Leena was grateful she'd found someone to listen to her. Even so, she'd do her own investigating when he wasn't around. She'd make mental notes of everything they talked about, especially when he took her to the crime scene.

The plan was to have Roger return two nights from now to take her to the warehouse. Currently, time would be spent arranging her aunt's memorial service. Her aunt requested cremation with her ashes to be kept in an urn at the psychic shop. Leena wasn't comfortable with graves or urns but for her aunt, she'd do anything.

Laziness filled her, so she sat thinking of how to give her aunt a proper ceremony. The truth was she knew she had to organize the service, but had no idea who to contact. She didn't know who her aunt's friends were, even though Roger would've helped, she wanted all his attention on the murder. Someone pounded on the door, startling her.

"What now?" She didn't really want to talk to anyone…too much crap to do.

If I just sit here and don't answer, will they go away?

The pounding repeated, becoming more forceful. "Nope."

She opened the door to a large very attractive blonde woman dressed in only what she could describe as gypsy clothing. It reminded her of the few pics she had of her mother's family. Her hair was piled on the back of her head with curls draping down and a large scarf tied around it all. The woman's face spread into a huge grin as Leena stared in disbelief.

"You're the spitting image of your mother. At least the pictures Addie showed me of her. Hi, Baby Girl, I came as soon as Addie contacted me, telling me you needed help with all of this mess."

She pounced on the girl, wrapping her arms around her and hugging her tight. "How're you doing?"

Leena panicked at the thought of being suffocated. The woman's chest was massive and surrounded her entire face. It was like being buried. She tried not to push away from her but couldn't help it.

"Um, who're you?" she asked pulling away from the woman's hold.

"Oh child, I'm sorry. I'm Madame Lillian Day, but everyone calls me Miss Lilly. I run the occult shop and brothel two blocks down from Jackson Square. Addie was my best friend and she talked about you all the time. Night before last, we all met for dinner, and your aunt was excited you came to visit. She hoped you'd move in and stay. She loved you very much."

Tears pooled in Leena's eyes and she stepped back before the woman hugged her again. "Please, come in. I was trying to decide how to organize her memorial service."

"It's exactly why I'm here. Addie told me you'd need my help so here I am. I'll help you with everything. We can rent a spot at the New Orleans City Park and set up a table for her urn and a picture. She just had one made...I bet it's in her bedroom. We can have chairs placed around for those who need them, but most people will bring blankets to sit on the ground. It's very informal and laid back. The weather's been perfect so it should be a beautiful memorial."

"Miss Lilly? What do you mean Addie told you?"

"Exactly what I said, sweetie. I was doing a reading for myself and she spoke to me."

"Through the Tarot?"

"No, silly, I could hear her. She said to tell you not to worry because she's watching over you. And expect her lawyer to contact you by the end of the week."

The girl's face was puzzled but decided against questioning her further.

"Can I get you anything to drink? I've got coffee, sweet tea, water, and cola...please, sit."

"I'll take sweet tea with ice if you have some made."

"I do."

Truth be told, Leena was glad for the distraction. She'd been consumed with the murder. Waiting to visit the crime scene was driving her nuts. Lilly was mumbling something to her as she poured the tea into a glass of ice. She set the glass in front of her and sat down.

"When were you planning to have the memorial, dear?"

"I'm not sure. I'll have her ashes sometime tomorrow and I'd like to have it as soon after as possible."

"Perfect. We can have it day after tomorrow. I'll make all the arrangements and you won't need to lift a finger. I loved Addie and it would be an honor for me to do this for you."

"I appreciate it. Since I'm new here, I wouldn't have known who to contact."

"Have the police said any more about the murder?"

"I haven't heard anything since they initially came to tell me. They were waiting on the autopsy results. One of the detectives agreed to take me to the crime scene after her memorial."

"Why on earth would he do that?"

"Simple. I told him I'd go by myself if he didn't agree to."

"Why child?" She watched the woman's face scrunch up in bewilderment.

"I want to get a feel for the murder. See if I can pick up any vibes or find any other clues. I'm determined to find out who did this and why. The detective asked if my aunt was into BDSM. I told him no but I really have no idea if she participated or didn't."

"Years ago, she'd been active, but not lately. She did keep up with her friends at one of the local dungeons. But she hadn't played in a long time."

She tried to hide the shock on her face. "Wow, you just never know." The more she thought about her aunt in black leather, the more she uncontrollably giggled. "Way to go, Nana."

"Did she tell you she hoped you'd help her in the shop?"

"Yeah, she mentioned something about it. We took a tour through the place and she told me she lost her sales person."

"Her business had gotten really swamped. She hoped you'd kept up with your card reading so you could let her take a break once in a while."

"She told me. I'm nowhere near the level as her, but I told her I'd try if she gave me a refresher course."

"Addie was the best. She didn't believe in bull shitting around or puffing the clients with false hope. Simply straight forward readings for her business. You know, I'd be happy to give you some pointers, but I'm in the same boat as you. I'm no Addie. I've talked your ear off enough…time for me to go. Now don't you worry about a thing. It'll be ready day after tomorrow and will be a beautiful service. Do you have a pen handy?"

The girl reached across to the counter and grabbed a pencil from a cup. Handing the pencil to Lilly, she pulled a piece of paper out of the pocket of her skirt and wrote a group of numbers on it.

"This is my phone number. You call me if you need anything. Even if it's just to talk. You hear me?"

"Yes, Lilly, thank you."

****

She sat on a blanket thinking how beautiful the park was. The moss hung off the trees giving the park a relaxed and dreamy feel. Everything had gone as planned over the past two days. Miss Lilly was a Godsend or maybe she should say an Addie-send. No matter, the woman had come through for her and she was grateful.

The photograph of her aunt was placed next to the urn on a small table covered with a lace cloth. Her eyes focused on Addie's face. Various friends gave heartfelt thoughts about her but Lilly's was the one who brought tears to Leena's eyes. The woman truly loved and missed her friend. She closed her eyes.

I miss you, Nana. I'd just found you and now you've been taken away. What do I do now? I can't leave until your estate is settled. I'm not even sure I want to leave. Oh Nana, I feel so lost. I want whoever did this to pay.

'Nonsense child, you're not lost and certainly never alone. I sent Lilly to you. She'll keep you grounded and encouraged. Find the one who did this so I can rest knowing you're safe.'

As quickly as the voice had spoken, it was gone. The girl's eyes flashed open, searching the group for anyone who heard what she did. Everyone was intently listening to the last speaker.

Over by the trees, she spotted Roger. He observed the group, studying them one at a time. She had a perfect view of him from her spot on the ground. He wasn't on duty and must have known the casual atmosphere of most memorials because in her opinion, his dress was hot. She'd never really allowed herself to study him, since he'd always been focused on business and had his partner with him. The man was casually leaning his upper body against the trunk of a tree with his arms crossed over his chest. His long sleek body looked really good in the light blue pinstriped dress shirt. Especially since the top two buttons were left open and his sleeves were rolled up almost to his elbows. Her lungs gasped for breath when her eyes moved down his hip hugging stone-washed jeans, all the way to his crossed ankles.

Dear God, how did I miss this before?

Of course he didn't wear socks, showing off his slightly dark hair covered ankles.

Damn, look at that tan.

He had a confident and alert stance…all things which were part of his detective nature she supposed. Her eyes roamed back to his face. His hair was brown with reddish highlights. It was cut a little long but short enough to meet regulations. It was tousled and free, not plastered down like most men in the work force. Strong forehead, cheeks, and chin framed his piercing brown eyes. She could get lost in those eyes if she let herself.

Still staring into those soulful eyes, she was mortified when they turned, gazing straight into hers. He cocked an eyebrow and smiled at her. Startled, she turned her head but not before she saw the bulge in his tight jeans. Her face had to be red because it was hot as hell from his big revelation.

When the speaker finished, everyone was dismissed. She stood by the table greeting those wishing to offer condolences. She'd no idea the crowd was as big as it was…she'd never turned around to look. Her aunt had so many friends. Off in the distance, Roger turned and ambled toward the street. She actually felt sad he didn't come by. But then, why would he? He and his partner had never met her aunt.

By the time all the people had filed by, the park had been picked up and everything packed away. Lilly dropped her back at home, making sure she understood she could call anytime day or night. Not ready to go through the shop quite yet to reach the living quarters, she took the outside stairs.

Once inside she secured all of the locks her aunt had installed on the door and then hit the button on the answering machine. As the first message started, she placed her Nana's urn on the kitchen cabinet. The message was from the lawyer, asking for confirmation of her appointment to go over the will tomorrow morning.

The last message was from Roger, stating he'd pick her up at seven this evening to go to the warehouse. He reminded her to wear comfortable clothing.

As if I own any other kind.

She looked at her watch realizing it was three in the afternoon, giving her enough time for a nap. Stretching out on the couch, she drifted off gazing at her aunt's face. Of course, it was only a dream and a troubled one at that. Strapped to a crossbeam of a building, a dark silhouette came toward her carrying a dagger dripping blood. Something was burning her...a pain in her wrists. Looking down, she'd been cut and was dripping blood. Panic set in and she struggled to break free of her bonds. As the figure stood over her, she was shocked awake by loud pounding.

Chapter Three

The effects of the nightmare, along with the pounding on the door, freaked her out. She jumped up from the couch and ran toward the door.

I really need to install a doorbell.

Squinting through the peephole, she recognized Roger and began the tedious task of unlocking every lock.

"Looks like I woke you. Are you sure you still want to go? We can always go tomorrow." Roger strolled in and sat at the kitchen table. She spotted he had the same sexy clothes on.

"All I need to do is change clothes; it won't take me long." She left him and sauntered to her bedroom. Jeans and a sweatshirt were at the top of a pile of clothes by the door into the bathroom. She grabbed them off the pile as she managed her way to the toilet, quickly stripping off her skirt and top. Once dressed, she slipped her feet into boots, grabbed a jacket, and went back into the kitchen.

"I'm ready…let's go."

He stood in front of her brushing his index finger down her cheek. "You sure about this?"

"Yes, Roger, I'm very sure. Either shut up and take me, or stay here and I'll call a taxi."

Throwing both hands in the air, he took a step back. "No…no, I'll take you." She giggled at his fake display of surrender. They ran down the steps to the street and she looked around to find his car. Not knowing what he drove, she stood there looking at him with a grin across his face.

"I drive the red Dodge Challenger." She watched him punch the key fob, unlocking the doors.

The ride to the warehouse was quiet. Her nerves were on edge at what she'd find, or maybe there wouldn't be any clues to find. When he pulled up in front of the building, Leena just sat there staring at the crime scene tape stretched across the door.

"I'll be with you the entire time. I won't let you out of my sight." His voice was sincere and reassuring. The minute she crossed the barrier tape, she felt cold and panic set in. Her steps were slow moving into the warehouse and as promised he stayed right at her side.

The electricity had been turned on in the abandoned building in order for the police to do their investigation at night, as well as in the day. Roger flipped a switch on the wall bringing everything into view. She staggered inside, shocked; there was very little in the warehouse. Her feet stopped in the center of the room and she turned slowly in a circle viewing everything. The Saint Andrew's cross was in the far corner of the huge room and was the only thing in it besides a few boxes stacked at the opposite end.

"It's the only thing in here?"

"I told you, it was abandoned years ago. Whoever did this used this building as a onetime showplace."

"And what kind of clues did you find?" Agitation and anger rolled through her mind.

"There were hardly any clues left. No prints were found, no blood, except on the blade of the dagger, and below it where it'd dripped on the concrete. And the blood was identified as your aunt's. The only thing we did find were tire tracks left in the dust on the concrete, leading through the door and up to the cross. We were able to get excellent photographs of the tire tread, hopefully to determine a make and model of the vehicle he or she used."

Not saying a word, she turned away from him, slowly inching her way to the cross. This was where her Nana breathed her last breath. Leena's heart ached thinking of her aunt feeling the pain of a slow death.

Yes, it had to be a slow death because a fast one would have been incredibly messy and impossible to clean up.

She approached the cross with reverence. Closing her eyes, she grabbed hold of one of the chains used to confine her aunt's arm. Her body jolted and immediately she transported into the crime scene with her aunt.

Fear. Oh God, I feel fear.

Roger tried to comfort her but she didn't answer him. She was immersed in the vision, during the time the murder occurred. The killer was tall, broad and stocky in build. He wore a hoodie with the hood pulled over his head. His face was impossible to see. He wore surgical gloves, not the cheap kind you could get at any store, which ripped when putting them on. No, he wore the expensive kind which protect the surgeon's skin.

Her aunt's naked body was chained to a St. Andrew's cross. Rather than chain her aunt's arms over her head, he confined them in a downward position. The girl let her eyes look down at her aunt's feet and saw a thick tarp had been placed under the cross.

He stepped up to her Nana and she observed he wore thick steel-toed work boots. He had a dagger in his hand and sliced it across the old woman's wrist. She whimpered and began to cry from the pain. Immediately, he placed a thick baggie over her hand and above the cut. Then he sealed it around her arm with surgical tape. He collected her blood, letting it drain into the baggie. He repeated the same routine on the other wrist, and then stood back as if to admire his work.

Her aunt was sobbing by this time and Leena tried to calm her. Shocked to the point of nausea, she watched him slice her jugular and insert a tube attached to a bag. The blood flowed easily through the tubing. Before Leena became violently ill, her aunt turned looking straight into her niece's eyes.

"Stop him. Find him before it's too late for the rest."

Her body jerked, throwing her back when her hand let go of the chain. Roger grabbed her around the waist to keep her from falling to the floor. That's when he stared at her as if she had two heads.

"Leena. Your eyes...how did they do that?"

"Do what?" she whispered.

"They're green, bright green. Your eyes weren't the same color when we walked in here."

"You're right...they weren't. They change colors when, um, when I have visions."

"Visions?" His voice cracked when he repeated her word.

"Yes, Roger, I have visions and when I do, my eyes turn a very bright green. Don't you laugh or say one negative word about it. I've put up with my family calling me the spawn of Satan all of my life. Nana was the only one who believed and understood me."

His arms went around her supporting her body and securing her once more. "No, darling, I'd never make fun of you. I believe you. Let's get you home…this has taken a lot out of you."

Her legs wobbled trying to hold up her trembling body.

It's a good thing he's holding on to me. I don't think I'm going to make it.

He guided her through the taped barrier across the door. The cool air washed over her, buckling her body until she slumped to the ground. Her chest heaved, trying to force something from her stomach which was long gone.

She had the dry heaves. Control of her body was no longer an option and her gut surged upward, spewing bile over the ground. Barely able to catch her breath, the hurling continued until her stomach was totally empty.

Roger took the front tail of his shirt and cleaned her mouth. Then he picked her up and carried her to the car.

****

He laid her in the back seat of the car covering her with the jacket she brought.

God, she's so sick. Whatever she saw messed her up but good.

Satisfied she was comfortable and solidly positioned on the backseat, he slammed the door and ran around to the driver's side.

Jumping Jack Flash played from the front pocket of his pants. He dug in his pocket grabbing his phone, checking caller ID. His partner's name was displayed.

"Bryan, man, I'm glad you called. I need help. Can you meet me at Leena's place? She's sick and I need help getting her into her apartment. Thanks, I owe you."

The door popped open after hitting the fob again, and he slid behind the steering wheel. He took off, squealing his tires. Definitely not following the speed limit signs, he took the side roads, missing the pedestrian traffic in the streets. Fifteen minutes later, he pulled in front of the shop. Bryan was standing, waiting on him.

Roger searched her pockets for the key to the apartment. He handed them to his partner and then reached in the back lifting her off the seat. Step by step, he carefully carried her up the stairs and through the open door.

"I could swear this is what she looked like the last time I saw her." Bryan was shaking his head.

"Yeah, she had another shock tonight. Hey, look in the fridge and cabinets for crackers and a soda or juice, would you?"

"Hang on." One door after another slammed as his partner went through every cabinet. "She's got crackers but I don't see any cola or juice."

"Can you run down to the corner and get some apple juice?"

His partner sighed. "Okay. I'll be back in a minute."

Roger carried her into her bedroom gently laying her on her bed. He started to turn toward the door when her hand gripped his arm.

"No, please stay with me."

He couldn't resist the look on her face. "I'm here, baby." As soon as the word baby left his lips, he regretted saying it. Not because he wouldn't love for her to be his baby, but because he didn't want to scare her away. "Can you tell me about it yet, Leena?"

She rolled over on her side facing him. "You won't believe me, Roger."

"Try me." He listened as she went through everything she saw. Silence filled the room when she finished. He squeezed her hand trying to reassure her, but she let go turning her face away.

"I told you, you wouldn't believe me."

"Hey, I didn't say a word. I'm simply thinking through the details you told me."

"That's the point. You didn't say anything."

"Turn around here and look at me. Now." He waited until she followed his orders. "Don't presume to know what my silence means. I believe you saw something. I saw your body react from the minute you touched the chain. You can't fake that kind of freak out. Plus, those details weren't released to the public. We knew he had to have collected the blood into something else but weren't sure what."

Bryan came back with apple juice. He poured a glass and brought a sleeve of crackers into her.

"Can I talk to you a minute?"

Roger reassured her he'd only be gone a minute.

"I'm heading for home. Did you believe the crap she spewed?" Bryan had his hands in his pockets, fumbling for his keys.

"Yeah, I did. I was there and saw how her body reacted. No way she could fake the sweats, fast pulse, and fear to that extreme. She believes she saw something and it scared the shit out of her."

"You're digging in a little deep here, sport."

"I'm not. The girl lost her aunt for Christ's sake. Give her a fucking break."

"Okay…okay. I'm just saying. I'll see you at the station in the morning."

Bryan gave her door keys back to Roger before he turned to leave. Once he left, he strolled back into her bedroom. She was eating crackers and sipping on the juice. A bit of her color spread back across her skin. He sat down, smiling at her.

"Your partner thinks I'm whacked."

"Doesn't matter what he thinks. He wasn't there. I was and I believe you. What was that thing you did?"

"You mean the visions? Sometimes depending on the person or circumstance, I'll touch someone or something they've touched and I'll see things. Things in their past, present, or future. I never know how it'll hit me. My dad was a preacher and he, along with his congregation, tried to exorcise me when I was ten. I'm not possessed, so of course, it didn't work. Nana always told me I was gifted and should use it to help others. She went through hell, Roger, and I'm going to find the person who did it."

She closed her eyes while he sat beside the bed and watched her. Her life had been lonely and rough, but it didn't affect her beauty outside or inside. After a few minutes her breathing slowed down. Her muscles occasionally gave involuntary twitches. She'd fallen asleep but he stayed to make sure she fell into a deep sleep. Once satisfied, he bent over and kissed her forehead, then quietly left.

Chapter Four

Leena's alarm blared, jolting her out of her dreams. Her hand slammed the button on the clock turning the music off.

I don't need that this early in the morning.

The room had a chill to it and she wanted to stay under the covers where it was toasty. Once more she looked at the clock, realizing she had an hour before her appointment. Slowly sitting upright, she moaned as her legs slid off the bed and her feet hit the floor. Last night had been too damn much for her. She showered, dressed, and sat at the kitchen table eating a left over croissant. Plans to investigate her Nana's murder filled her mind, and she needed someone to help her. Someone who knew the BDSM scene, along with a few of the other clubs. Last night's vision gave her the impression it was someone active in New Orleans' night life, as well as someone who was knowledgeable in medical procedures.

Roger wouldn't help her. She figured he'd try to use his detective muscle to keep her out of it. Lilly would be a great help and she'd be willing too. She'd stop by her shop after meeting with the lawyer.

Since the lawyer's office was in the downtown business district, she called a taxi to take her, rather than walk. The envelope with the address was in her purse as well as Lilly's business card. It was time for her to start this.

The taxi dropped her at one of the older, renovated buildings, near the newer high rise buildings downtown. The lawyer was on the fifth floor. She stepped out into a huge room which reminded her of a fancy check-in area of a plush hotel. Glittering cut glass chandeliers and lamps, gray plush carpets, expensive furniture in burgundy, and what appeared to be a buffet table filled with pastry, filled the room. She checked in at the receptionist desk and turned to find a chair. Several clients were sitting in chairs already waiting.

Wow, I'm underdressed. Everyone here looks as if they stepped out of a Vogue magazine spread. Where on earth did Nana find this guy, and how could she afford him?

Before Leena could sit, the secretary called her name.

"Ms. Adaleena Price, Mr. Stevenson will see you now. Please follow me."

Her face cringed at the use of her full name. If only she'd worn a dress instead of her jeans, but she'd have to make the best of it. After all, she wasn't here to make a good impression. The secretary led her to an office at the end of the hall and introduced her upon entering.

"Mr. Bradly Stevenson, Miss Adaleena Price."

"Miss Price, please, have a seat. Can I get you a drink before we start? We have juice, bottled water, coffee, or cola."

Her eyes took a quick survey of the handsome man dressed in a three piece suit, shaking her hand as she sat on his fancy, leather straight backed chair.

"No, thank you, I just finished breakfast before I came. I'm fine."

His eyes were the color of a summer sky after it'd rained and cleared the air. Long, but neatly trimmed locks of golden hair fell around his face, perfectly framing it. From his broad shoulders and trim waist she could tell he did some sort of athletics. Plus, his tan was hard to miss. His body suddenly stopped and she noticed everything was quiet. She looked up at his staring eyes, realizing she never heard a word of what he'd said to her.

"I'm so sorry. Can you please repeat it? I'm afraid my mind was somewhere else."

"I'm sure this is overwhelming for you. I was just asking about your name, Adaleena. It's a lot like your aunt's name, Addie. What an amazing and extremely colorful person. I'm sorry for your loss."

"Yes, she was, Mr. Stevenson. I was named after her…my mother and she were friends."

"Ah, it explains a lot. Let's get down to business, shall we? I had the greatest respect for your aunt and through the years, she designated me as executor of her estate should anything happen. I've been through her financial statements versus any outstanding debt and her estate is worth over nine hundred thousand dollars, after my commission and taxes. I realize the circumstances aren't the best, but being of sound mind and body, she left it all to you."

Leena sat back against her chair with her hand on her chest, trying to catch her breath. She couldn't believe what she'd just heard. She'd no idea her aunt had that kind of money.

The lawyer smiled at her. "Your aunt, although eccentric in nature, was a frugal and shrewd business woman. And she's excellent at her craft, having a very large client base. I don't tell everyone this, but I've been going to her for a few years for her advice. The woman was gifted and a wonderful friend."

Tears pooled behind her eyes and even though she couldn't speak, she knew he understood.

"Do you have any idea what you're going to do now everything is settled?" he asked.

"No, Mr. Stevenson, I haven't quite thought that far ahead. I simply wanted to get through today."

"Please, call me Bradly. Mr. Stevenson is my father."

All the necessary papers were filled out and she signed them as he helped her go through each one. He rose from behind his desk and held her hand as he explained everything was now legally in her name, including the bank accounts.

"If I can be of any further assistance, please don't hesitate to call me. I will from time to time, check on you, with your permission of course."

Flustered and surprised, she smiled and answered, "I look forward to it Mr....oops, Bradly. Thank you for all your hard work and for taking care of my Nana."

She left the office, hailed a cab, and headed straight for Lillie's.

****

Roger and Bryan sat at their desks at the precinct discussing the evidence taken from the crime scene, what little there was. To say they were frustrated was an understatement.

"I can't believe the only evidence we have is the tread marks. This is bullshit. No one is smart enough not to leave *something* behind. The only real information we have is that it was a large enough truck to haul heavy equipment, possibly a crane. Dammit, do you know how many of those trucks are in the New Orleans area alone, not to mention the suburbs and surrounding areas."

"Now hang on there, Bry, we've got more than that." It had been a week since the murder and Roger tried hard to keep his partner cool and focused on facts. "Although we can't pin down a make and model, we do know it was a truck. And the fact is, once the truck drove into the warehouse and stopped, jacks were deployed, lifting the truck off the floor. Square marks were by the tire marks. I'm figuring he hauled the cross in there and with an attached crane, lifted and placed it where we found the body. We also know the perpetrator was probably experienced with medical procedures and had access to equipment. He knew how to place the tubing into the jugular to speed the draining of her body. No ordinary man on the street would be able to do it. Then there's the strong connection with the BDSM community. We're not totally in the dark, my friend."

"What's your take on the niece? You know I dug into her background. Her father was one of those holy-roller preachers. Her mother's family were all gypsies and traveled around. She ran away from home when she was fifteen. It was presumed she went to live with them. You think she's legit?"

"After seeing what I saw...yeah, I have no doubt."

"Are you sure you're not just giving in to your attraction to her? It's obvious she's made a huge impression on you."

"Yeah, I'm attracted to her, but I'm not so blinded by it I'd deliberately ignore facts of the case, or overlook anything she's involved in. Shit went down last night I don't even begin to understand but I believe her. I intend to stay close."

"Uh huh."

****

Lilly's store was eight blocks away from her aunt's. The taxi dropped her off in front of a large five story, red brick building which was as wide as two store fronts. She stood in front looking up to the top floor and almost lost her balance. The neon sign in the front window displayed Madame Lilly's House of Mystical Love. Leena shook her head and giggled before she stepped through the front door.

Her senses went into overload simply by walking into the place. A sensor must have been in the floor, because the minute she crossed through the door, a buzzer sounded and two employees approached her. Aromatherapy enveloped her nose, eliciting several emotional and memory reactions in her. A male and female approached her asking if she needed any help. The female was dressed provocatively in a low cut bustier, matching garter belt, hose, and stilettos. She knew which side of the store this little lady worked. The male, dressed in a gypsy style fashion, so she knew he worked this side of the store. She thanked both of them but declined their help, stating she needed to see Lilly. The lady crossed through the doorway covered with strings of beads into the brothel side of the building.

Leena turned her eyes to the decorum of the room. The lighting was extremely subdued making it hard to see. She managed to detect various sizes and types of crystals, bottles and jars containing various powders and liquids, crystal balls, tarot cards, cloths to cover the table where fortunes were read…every item you could imagine a fortune teller or witch would need to practice her craft or religion. The walls were painted a dark maroon, trimmed in gold. Books of *How to* were stacked on shelves behind the counters. The variety of items was amazing. At the far end of the room was another doorway covered in long strings of beads, separating one room from the other. It intrigued her as she inched her way toward it. She intended to peek in once she discretely arrived at the doorway, but suddenly Lilly popped through the beads reaching out her arms to hug her.

Luckily, she didn't hug her very long.

"Hi Lilly. I stopped in to see your store and also ask you a favor."

The large woman escorted her through the beads and offered her a seat at her mystic table. She didn't use a crystal ball but her tarot cards were stacked on a black silk cloth covering the table.

"What can Miss Lilly do for you, baby?"

"I want to investigate my aunt's murder, separate from the homicide detectives. It isn't that I lack trust in them, they simply don't have the tools I do." She proceeded to tell the old woman what had transpired at the warehouse when she went there. Also, she shared her aunt's plea to stop him before it was too late. Leena felt sure it was a warning there would be more murders.

"I want you to take me to the BDSM club where Nana used to frequent. I want to meet the people she interacted with. Also, I want to look into the human vampire element in New Orleans since this guy bled her to death. I'm not really sure they had anything to do with it but I'd at least like to talk with a few of them…and I need your knowledge of the city and the night life in it. Will you help me, Lilly, for my Nana?"

The woman sat back in her chair appearing to scrutinize Leena, while crossing her arms across her chest under her very large breasts. Finally, she sat straight and let out a large sigh.

"I will on two conditions. Number one is you listen and follow my instructions carefully when we go into these clubs and visit. No arguing with me…what I say goes. Number two is you report back to those two detectives everything we discover. I want them aware of what we're doing in order for you to be protected. Will you agree to those terms?"

She didn't want to say yes but she understood anything else and the woman would never help her. "I agree."

"On both of them?" Lilly asked.

"Yes, on both."

"Good. I'll make the arrangements and understand, we will take our time doing these so-called investigations of yours…not all at once. Now tell me what happened at the lawyer's appointment."

"Where on earth did Nana find him? He's good looking and hot…not at all what I thought he'd be. Basically, the estate is settled and her business and all her assets were left to me. I never knew she was such a fantastic entrepreneur. She's a very surprising woman and it's no wonder I loved her so much."

"Wonderful. Do you have any idea what you'll do with the building?"

"I'm thinking about keeping the shop open, hiring someone to clerk the occult shop, while I read fortunes for those clients who decide to stay with us. I'll need help refreshing myself but it shouldn't take very long. I've tried to keep up with it. Actually my gift may offer more insight into the clients than my cards will."

"That's good news, dear, think of what you can do with all the money. New clothes, a car, better apartment…what fun it would be."

"No, Lilly, I'm not touching the money except to pay the utilities."

"She left it to you, Darlin. I know it's what she meant it for."

"I know, Lilly, but I also know how much she loved her shop. No, the money won't be spent on anything but necessities for Addie's Mojo."

"Well, I'll help you anyway I can, love. Don't you worry about a thing. There's enough people working under me I can spend a few hours a day away from my shop. And yes, child, Bradly is an exceptionally sensual man. If I were younger I'd take him to my many rooms upstairs, if you know what I mean. Addie met him at the BDSM club. He's a Dom there and was good friends with her. The man can definitely dominate. Give me a couple of days to set things up and I'll give you a call. In the meantime, take a couple of days and familiarize yourself with the inventory in your shop. Let me show you the wilder side of my building."

Leena was in awe when she crossed the threshold, surrounded by red velvet which lined the walls and floor. The furniture was plush white velvet with many red throw pillows. Her eyes were huge taking it all in.

"My God, Lilly, what did I just walk into?"

Chapter Five

Roger tossed and turned the entire night. Bits of Leena's vision mixed with his own dreams and created a never ending chase scene. He woke exhausted and frustrated at not being able to subdue the culprit in his dreams.

At the last minute, he'd taken the day off to gather his thoughts and emotions. He surprised himself when he realized Bryan had truly pissed him off. His accusation of Roger not being able to distance his feelings for her from the crime, flew all over him.

The coffeemaker had been programmed to make a full pot before he ever got up. He poured a cup and took it out on the upstairs deck overlooking the city. A chill was in the air but after the night he had, it stimulated him and made him feel alive. The city was slowly waking, filling the streets with cars and people going about their business.

A few shops along his street were opening their doors for business as he sat sipping his coffee. His thoughts turned to Leena, wondering what she'd planned for the day. It'd been a couple of days since he'd checked on her. Maybe he'd go over and make sure she's doing okay or see if she needed anything. With each sip of his coffee, he talked himself into going.

The storekeeper across the street hollered his name and waved. Nodding, he finished his cup, stood, and stepped back into his apartment. It wasn't a fancy place but it suited his needs. Two bedrooms, two baths, kitchen and dining, and a large living room. It took up the entire top floor of the building which housed a local bakery. The aromas in the mornings made it hard for him not to gain a lot of weight. The owners were an older Italian couple who made the best bread in New Orleans, at least he thought so. Mama Tascal was always trying to arrange dates for him with her nieces or clients' daughter's. So far, he escaped her plans.

Rinsing his cup and placing it in the dishwasher, he turned on his heels, strutting to the shower. It was surprising how his mood lifted, simply knowing he was on his way to see her. He put on a pair of tight jeans with a long sleeved, black and white plaid shirt and a black wife beater T-shirt underneath. His Adidas Barricade tennis shoes were by the bed and he slipped them on and tied them. He'd dressed for comfort.

Rather than take the outside stairs, he took the ones inside, which exited through the bakery. Papa Tascal tossed him a hot scone on his way out the door. His car was parked on the street instead of behind the building in the lot.

I really was pissed off last night.

Most people in his neighborhood usually kept a watchful eye on his Challenger. They understood if anything happened to his baby, he'd be on the perp like a tick on a dog. He slipped behind the wheel, revving the engine until she purred.

Just the way I want to drive Leena.

****

She woke incredibly rested…first night she'd slept without nightmares. The only plans she had for the day consisted of going over inventory in the shop. She slipped on a pair of black leggings with an oversized red sweatshirt, falling just above her knees. Stepping into a pair of flip-flops, she made herself a cup of hot chocolate, since coffee tasted like mud. She grabbed the keys to the shop, her aunt's urn, and her cup of chocolate, heading to the inside staircase. The stairs were steep. Carefully taking them one by one, she reached the bottom with a huge sigh of relief. The thought of falling and spraying Nana's ashes into the air horrified her. She'd never forgive herself if she'd coated the stairwell with her aunt's DNA.

The door unlocked with a bit of effort on her part, and she flipped all the lights on letting her see everything. First thing she did was make a type of memorial behind the check-out counter and placed her aunt's urn on a shelf. Previously, she'd brought her aunt's photograph down and placed it on the same shelf, beside a vase of flowers. It looked perfect and her clients would be able to see it and remember her aunt.

The young girl turned a complete circle, surveying the entire shop, but not really knowing where to start. Only thing she could do, would be to jump right in and start listing items. She found a pad of paper and a pen stuffed in a drawer and started making lists of all the items in the glass case of the counter. Various pieces of jewelry were in the cases from pentagrams, Celtic, silver chains, and

Wiccan. She took a count of each item and wrote the total by its name. Once she finished there, she decided to open the shop to the outside world. That way, if any clients wanted to come in and shop, she'd be able to meet and greet them. She flipped the sign in the front window from closed to open, and unlocked the door.

Her body turned, scrutinizing the room, trying to decide where to take inventory next. There was a small room on the left, next to the wall with the book case. It held a long table with ten chairs and nothing else. Nana's psychic room was behind the counter to insure privacy.

What better place to start than with the books?

She moved in that direction, noticing the books were labeled with a category. Beginning, Intermediate, and Advanced Wicca, Candle Magic, Holistic Health, Dreams, Meditation, Earth Religions were but a few of the labels with at least five books in each division.

This is going to be a bigger job than I imagined. Was Nana into all of this?

Shelves on the other side of the small doorway contained candles of every shape, size, color, and purpose. Some smelled and some had no scent at all. There were labels for different groupings of candles such as seven day, prayer, image, herbal, and horoscope. The fact they had different uses baffled her.

Next to the candles were rows of incense followed by several shelves of crystals and gem stones. Everything had its purpose and name. She dutifully took a count of each one adding it to her list.

The last section on this particular wall of shelves was the Sacred Statuary. Goddesses and gods, Eqyptian goddesses and gods, Norse, fairy and fantasy were all labeled and in their spot. She'd remembered seeing a few statues scattered on top the glass counter up front.

A buzzer sounded making her turn to see four older women stroll into the shop. They were all smiling as they looked around the room.

"Are you open for business?" one asked.

"No, I'm afraid not. I hope to be up and running by next week. I left the door open, hoping to meet a few of my aunt's clients and friends. Did you know her?"

"You must be Leena. Yes, we all knew her very well and were saddened when we heard the news. Such a horrible tragedy," the same woman stated.

Three more people, possibly tourists, came in and browsed around the store. She repeated her speech about the store not being open for business, but assured them they were more than welcome to look around. Within thirty minutes, there were at least twenty people in the store and she couldn't keep track of them. Frustration and panic set in as she tried her best to keep up with them. Items were being touched and lifted in order to inspect them or look at a price. It happened so fast she would never know if anything had been pocketed.

The buzzer went off again and Leena thought she'd explode. Abruptly turning to see who it was, her eyes lit up when she saw Roger enter the shop. In a flash she asked if he would help corral everyone and send them out the door. It took fifteen minutes but they were finally successful. The blinds were pulled and door locked.

"Whew, worst mistake of my life. I'd no idea so many would come in here. I simply wanted to meet some of my aunt's clients and friends. Thank you for your help."

"You're welcome. Glad I could be of service."

"What are you doing here? Although, I'm grateful you are."

"I took the day off and wanted to check on you."

"Oh." Her heart fell a little. He just wanted to make sure she's doing okay, she told herself. She moved toward the back of the store near the cash register. He followed her keeping close.

"And…I simply wanted to spend time with you." The smile plastered on his face made her blush.

"You did? Why?"

"I like you. I want to know you better, that's all. I've no ulterior motives…I'm off the clock."

His smile almost made her speechless. She grinned up at him then lowered her eyes to the floor.

"It's awfully sweet of you. Thank you, Roger."

"Have you eaten? There's a burger joint around the corner which is good."

She'd been ready to give her answer, when his cell phone went off. He pulled it out of his jeans pocket looking at the Caller ID.

"I'm sorry, it's Bryan. I've got to take it."

While he argued with Bryan, she picked up several items off the counter and began putting them back on their shelf. Her hands grabbed two statues and she froze. Her body shivered, as prickling sensations flowed through her. She felt a familiar presence paralyzing her with fear. *It was him.*

Roger shut his phone off turning to apologize when he saw her pale face.

"Leena, what is it? What's wrong?"

She didn't look at him or even speak for several seconds. He placed his hands gently on her shoulders.

"Leena." She finally raised her eyes and answered.

"He was here…today. The killer was in this shop, Roger. He touched one of these statues. He knows who I am."

"How can you be sure?"

"When I picked up these two statues, I felt him. I saw what he saw, and he was watching me from across the room. He's smug, thinks he'd pulled one over on me being in Nana's shop."

"I've got to go into the precinct for a few minutes. Bryan called and insisted it was important. I'm not leaving you here alone so you're coming with me. We'll eat afterward."

"I can't simply leave. I've got to finish the inventory."

"You can and you will. No arguments. Let's make sure everything is locked up and we'll leave by the outside stairs."

The ride to the station was silent. She didn't want to talk, so she stared out her window as they passed by building after building. Really, she never saw them. She only saw his view of her talking with the others in the store. He was almost laughing at her. Her fear was quickly replaced by anger.

He drove the car into an underground parking garage and parked it next to the front elevator. They rode it up to the fourth floor where the homicide division was housed and Roger marched straight to Bryan.

"Okay, now tell me what was so urgent I had to come in for? I hardly ever take a day off and when I do, you always call me in."

Bryan looked to Leena. "I didn't know you were bringing her with you. I'm not sure it's a good choice."

"Well, we'd made plans to eat and I wasn't going to leave her high and dry. What's going on?"

"You need to see this." He then spoke to Leena. "You might want to have a seat out here."

"If this is about my aunt, I'm coming in? What've you found? I'm not leaving Roger's side."

"Suit yourself."

He led them into a back room where a plastic bag was lying on a table. He picked the bag up and handed it to Roger. What she saw when she looked at it made her skin crawl. Inside the bag was a sacred statue of a goddess similar to the one's sold at her shop. It was covered in blood.

"Whose blood is on it?"

"Your aunt's," answered Bryan.

Chapter Six

Leena couldn't take her eyes off the evidence bag in Roger's hands.

"Why don't you hold it? Maybe you'll get another vision and see his face, then we can put this crime to bed," Bryan snarled at her.

"What the fuck, man? Have you lost your mind? That's no way to talk to the victim's niece." Roger tossed the bag back to him and slid his arm around her shoulder.

"Sorry, Leena, I meant no disrespect. I'm going to log this in." Bryan left the room taking the evidence with him.

Her eyes fixed on him as he went out. On the verge of tears, she wondered what she'd done to make him distrust her so. Memories of her father smacked her again and she supposed he was like all the rest. He simply didn't believe her and assumed she'd made things up for the attention.

"Hey," she felt Roger's fingers lift her chin and her eyes up to his. "He lets these kinds of cases get to him...takes them personally. Are you still hungry?"

Sincerity poured out of his brown eyes when she studied them. He could be trusted. She'd felt it and knew she'd found someone who believed in her.

"Yes, I'm hungry. Can we still go for the burgers around the corner from my place?"

"You bet we can...come on."

They sat at the very back of the café, away from the noise and everyone else. His insight of knowing she needed time to compose herself from the shock of the statue, firmed her trust even more.

She ordered an onion cheeseburger while he'd ordered the jumbo Cajun burger. She snickered and teased him. "All those spices are going to tear your stomach up."

"Nah, I'm used to it. I love anything hot." He arched an eyebrow as a smile spread across his face.

Tingles ran through her body. She squirmed in her seat until she finally grabbed the dessert and drink menu to fan herself. His laughter roared through the back of the restaurant.

"Leena, I do believe you're blushing."

The heat rose even higher and she fanned faster. Thank God, the burgers arrived. Now she hoped he'd take his attention off her and put it on his food. The burger in front of her was piled high with shredded cheese and sautéed onions. Seasoned fries came with all burgers and her mouth hung open, inspecting the amount of food in front of her.

"I'm not going to be able to put my mouth around this big thing." Roger choked on his drink as she kept talking. "I can tell you right now, I'm going to need a box to take home the leftovers." Finally noticing he was staring at her with a huge grin across his face, she shook her head at him.

"What? What's wrong?"

"Not a thing, sweetness. I'm simply admiring your enthusiasm. You're a breath of fresh air."

Flustered, she smiled at him. "Stop, you're going to make me blush again."

"Nothing wrong with it. You're beautiful when you blush."

"Okay, change of subject...how long have you been a homicide detective?" Anything to get him to focus on something else was her goal. Her jaws popped wrapping around the burger, and onions slipped out of the buns falling into her lap. "Great."

Roger laughed again. "Here, let me help." His napkin was unused and he picked the onions out of her lap with it. Quiet broke out between them as their eyes met and held each other's. Grabbing another napkin, he wiped the escaping ketchup off her lips. Once again her body flushed. She wanted his lips on her, devouring her. If she leaned a little closer, it might coax him to do the same. Closer and closer they moved toward one another, when her phone suddenly played The Pointer Sisters song Jump, which she did.

"I'm sorry. It's Lilly and I need to check with her to see if our plans are still on for tonight."

Slowly, he moved back to his seat while she talked on the phone. The waitress brought their bill and he gave her his credit card, also asking for a box for her food.

After speaking with Lilly, she cut her burger in half, putting the uneaten portion into the box. Then she proceeded to finish the half she'd started on.

"You and Lilly have plans tonight?"

No way was she going to tell him her plans. He'd put a halt to her snooping around on her own.

"Um, yes. She's going to show me a little of the New Orleans' night life. We shouldn't be out too late."

"Well, then, I guess we'll wait for another time for me to show you around. Only if you're agreeable, that is."

"Oh, I'd love to. We've had this planned for days or I'd reschedule with her."

"It's okay. We'll get together another time. No worries."

The receipt and his card was placed in front of him and she watched him sign. Putting his card back in his billfold, he looked up and smiled at her. "Are you ready to go? I'll take you back so you'll have time to get ready. Oh, and I'm putting an unmarked car on you for twenty-four hour surveillance detail. Also, when you open for business, you'll have a uniformed policeman on duty inside of the store. It'll let the perpetrator know you're being watched and protected."

Laughter filled the car as they rode the short distance back to her apartment. It was easy for her to be around him. She believed she could tell him almost anything, except the fact she intended to investigate on her own. When he turned the engine off, they sat and talked for almost fifteen minutes about music, giving their opinions of who was the best. People strolling by would think they're simply friends enjoying an afternoon together.

"Well, I guess I'd better walk you up to your door. I enjoyed this afternoon very much. Don't worry about security, we'll keep you safe."

Once they were on the top landing, she dug in her purse for her keys and realized he was waiting for her to unlock the door. He followed her in, checking all the rooms and finally returned to stand in front of the door.

"Have fun tonight and be careful. Lilly knows the safe places, so I'm not too worried."

"Thank you for lunch and for taking such good care of me. I don't know what I'd have done without you."

"You're welcome, Baby Girl." He bent and kissed her on the forehead, then turned closing the door behind him. She locked the locks automatically and wondered why his calling her baby girl sent all sorts of electric tingles throughout her body. Then again, she really didn't need to wonder.

She hurried to her bedroom to change clothes, and decided against jeans and a t-shirt. Instead, she chose black leggings and a long tunic top. Black boots with four inch heels would be suitable for her feet. As she stepped back in the living room, she heard Lilly's trademark knock on her door.

****

Lilly took one look at Leena and knew she'd been right to bring the extra clothes.

"Oh, no, no, no, child. You can't wear those clothes to the Secret Whisper. They'd laugh us right back out the door. Here, put these on, and I don't want any argument. I chose the most modest outfit I had in the store. I hope you shave your girly bits. I never thought to ask until now."

Leena stood staring at her with her mouth open wide. She watched her eyes move from the top of her head down to the tip of her toes.

"Honey, if you thought we'd be able to get in to any of the dungeons in normal street wear, you thought wrong. I'm wearing what I normally play in at the club...they'd accuse me of losing my mind if I wore anything else. Now, hurry and change into the clothes I brought. If you have a long coat and would feel better in it until we get there, by all means, put it on."

She smiled as she watched the girl slowly turn and approach her bedroom door. She turned once, opened her mouth, and Lilly shook her head no.

Lilly made herself at home, adjusting her stockings, and then sat on the couch waiting for Leena to walk out for inspection. *Wait till she gets a look at what's under my skirt and blouse.* She chuckled just thinking about her face once they were at the club. She could tell by her reactions to everything, even though she'd lived on the streets for a time, her life was sheltered. This would be a new learning curve for her.

The door to the bedroom opened and a worried, beautiful young woman was standing in front of Lilly. Tears pooled in her eyes, as she gave the girl a huge smile.

"You're absolutely breathtaking, sweet girl. I couldn't have chosen a better outfit for you if I'd made it myself. It fits perfect and your beautiful eyes are glowing. Maybe with fear, but you'll get over it. Oh, good, you brought a coat, I see. It'll make you feel more secure until we get there. How are those stilettos working for you? I made sure they were the shortest ones I had. Are you ready to go? My car's parked down stairs in front of the store."

****

"What in the hell have I gotten myself into? I should've done this on my own...I can't wear this outside." She stood in front of her mirror in shock at what at the clothes she wore. Her eyes took in the soft teal colored bustier pushing her ample breasts up almost over the top of the black sequined lined edge. If she leaned over just right, she'd almost lose one of her breasts to the outside world. The bustier hugged her body to just above her belly button, where a gold angel piercing shined in the light. Grateful Lilly had chosen a modest pair of bottoms, though she still felt as if they showed too much. It was a satin pair of bottoms, cut in a high French cut, front and back.

Thank God, I shaved this morning. I'm shining like a bald monkey.

The color matched the bustier perfectly and the edges were also lined with black sequins. She felt like a marching band drum majorette, except for the black lace stockings and stilettos. She stepped back to look at the entire picture and was amazed. Her hair coloring and eyes shone bright against the teal. She really was beautiful.

I'm grabbing a coat anyway. Maybe they'll let me keep it on.

She strolled into the living room, with her coat thrown over her arm. Lilly teared up when she saw her. Leena felt herself blushing, when the woman told her how beautiful she was. She wanted to beg Lilly to change her mind, but the woman rushed her out the door, down to her car before she even spoke a word.

They were quiet while driving to the club. She hugged her coat close to her, and worried about everything from how little she wore, to the people there and how they'd react to her, and finally, to what she would see. She knew a little about BDSM. She'd had friends who were living the lifestyle and had wanted her to try it. But she'd had enough of a man bossing her around, keeping her sequestered from the world, and telling her she wasn't good for anything. She knew she wasn't dominant, but she didn't think she was submissive either, at least in her mind.

A large two story brick building loomed in front of them as Lilly pulled into a parking space right up front. It was dark and actually looked deserted.

"Now, I know what you're thinking…there really are people inside. All of the windows have been blacked out because of the nature of business inside. The fourth floor is private and the third floor is divided into rooms used for the special scenes and role playing. The second floor houses the reception desk and sign in, changing rooms, the owner's and managers' offices, a water and juice bar, and a dance floor with music for the meet and greet area, plus an occasional demonstration or two. The basement is considered our first floor and is the actual dungeon. This is where once paired with a Dom or sub, the actual play begins, unless either wants privacy. Then you must sign up and wait for a room on the third floor. Ready to go in?"

"Not really. I'm a bit terrified and embarrassed."

"You'll be fine, sweetie. Tonight you can stick close to me as my guest, unless of course, you find someone who stirs your heat."

"You're kidding, right?"

She watched her laugh, then was pulled up the few stairs, through the front door. A doorman/bouncer stood on the other side of the door, before entering into the receptionist area. Leena saw the two of them flirt unmercifully, and then they were ushered into the next area.

"Paul, this is my friend, Leena. She's my guest tonight and thinking of joining. I thought I'd show her around a bit and let her get the feel of the place. What paperwork does she need to fill out for you?"

"Hey, Miss Lilly, how's it going, babe? She just needs to fill out the basic information and financial statement, even though she hasn't joined yet. Also, she needs to fill out a soft/hard limit sheet in case she meets a D/s who interests her. There's also a sheet explaining the safe, sane, and consensual requirements, which also explain safe words and what we use. There's also a discussion on the proper behavior of a Dom or submissive, while on the premises."

He turned his face toward Leena and spoke directly to her. "Beautiful, we're privileged you chose us to check us out for membership. Miss Lilly is one of our faithful members and she'll show you the ropes. If you've any questions she can't answer, find one of the House Doms or myself and feel free to ask. You can finish filling out the forms while you're changing in our dressing rooms. Enjoy yourself, honey, and maybe you and I can meet up a little later."

She pulled her coat a little tighter around her body as she gave him a weak smile. He in turn gave her a big smile and wink. She followed Lilly into the first dressing room they came to, and shut the door behind them. She sat down on the couch, began finishing filling out the forms, and reading the material.

Once she finished, she looked up and her eyes popped. In front of her was Lilly, dressed in a solid black, leather bustier which squeezed her more than voluptuous breasts up to the top. Her nipples barely peeked over the edge. Even though the older blonde had ample curves, her body was toned and solid. She wore solid black pantyhose with a leather thong over them. Completing the outfit were thigh-high leather stiletto boots. The woman was amazing and hot, swinging a leather crop.

Chapter Seven

"Lilly?"

"Yes, child, what's wrong?"

"Are you…um, are you a Domme?" Leena kept staring at the woman's outfit wondering what in the hell she'd gotten herself into. This situation was quickly getting out of control.

"Yes, I am, Baby Girl and tonight you're *my* submissive. You're to stay close to me, keep your head and eyes down at all times, unless I tell you it's safe to look up. We have to look the part, darlin, if we're to blend in. They know me here and I'll say I'm showing you around, testing your experience. If a Dom speaks to you, you're to call him Sir. The owner of the establishment is to be addressed as Master and I'll let you know if he approaches. Don't raise your face unless the Dom tells you that you can. Have you got it all?"

"I think so, yes."

"I'll help you out if you forget. Now give me your coat and let's get out of here. The sooner we walk around, the faster we can gain information. Take your paperwork back to Paul and then come to my side. I won't make you kneel at my feet. I rarely do with a first time submissive."

Leena reluctantly removed her coat, handing it to Lilly's waiting hands. She felt naked without it but was grateful her outfit was at least covering her essential parts. However, it wasn't going to be difficult for her to keep her eyes down. Majorly embarrassed, she didn't want anyone to look at her.

She handed her papers to Paul, keeping her eyes on the desk until she turned to walk to her friend.

"Hey, beautiful, look up here at me. There you go." A sensuous smile was plastered across his face as he brushed his finger down her cheek. "Any chance I'll see you after I get off work?"

Suddenly, Lilly slapped her thigh with the crop.

"Come here, Baby Girl. She's mine to instruct tonight, Paul. Maybe another night."

"Okay, Miss Lilly. I'll hold you to it. You and Baby Girl enjoy the facilities."

Warm breath hit her ear as the woman leaned down and whispered. "He likes you, Leena. He's reading through your paperwork right now. Ready? Here we go."

Leena groaned under her breath.

The older woman led her over to the juice bar. She bought a bottle of water and one of apple juice. She thrust the bottled water into Leena's hand.

"Hang on to it. You'll need it before the night is over. You need to keep hydrated no matter what does or doesn't happen. Let's head down to the dungeon and walk through. We'll watch a few scenes so you can understand what goes on here and so I can get the feel of the place tonight. Also, I need to know who's here that I can talk to."

"Yes, Mistress."

"Very good, my dear. I'll make a sub out of you yet." She heard the woman chuckle and gulped in dread.

They spent a full thirty minutes simply walking by various scenes. The woman stopped near a scene, where a submissive bound to a St. Andrew's cross, was being flogged by her Dom. A small crowd had gathered to watch. Miss Lilly stood next to another Dom who was observing the couple.

"Baby Girl, I want you to raise your eyes and study this couple while I talk with my friend. Pay close attention to the Dom's wrist, as he flicks the flogger across her back and ass. Also, pay attention to the pattern he makes on her body. You'll be amazed."

She raised her head, staring intently at the scene being played out across from them. Right now, Leena wasn't impressed. She experienced embarrassment for the poor girl who stood naked in front of a room full of people. It wasn't something she would ever be able to do no matter who she trusted. Both participants had their backs to her. The tall Dom was shirtless, and his leather pants hung on his hips, hugging his very sensual ass. Even though his back was to her, she still had a good vantage point to watch his wrist. With each lift of the flogger, the muscles in his shoulders rippled and then flexed. His skin was tanned and sweat glistened on his back. She licked her lips but shook it off as she turned her attention to his wrist. He flicked the flogger with fluid motion sending the straps across the woman's back directly under the last set. The pink stripes were perfectly laid out in evenly spaced rows, and she had to admit they were beautiful. The woman moaned each time the leather impacted her skin, but it was hardly a moan of pain. Her orgasm was fast approaching, or at least it's what it sounded like to Leena. She'd never watched anything so intimate. Her body was aroused enough to make her nervous someone would be able to tell.

The Dom moved behind his sub, slowly running his fingers between her legs. Leaning close to her ear, Leena breathlessly watched him whisper into it. *God, I wish I knew what he said to her.* Before she realized, he'd lowered his leathers and thrust up against the woman's ass. He continued this until both bodies went rigid, then collapsed against the cross. Feeling as if she were spying, she lowered her head.

"It appears Mistress Lilly, your sub is uncomfortable watching public sex."

"Yes, Master James, it was one of her hard limits. She prefers the private rooms."

He strolled over and stood in front of Leena, lifting her head with his index finger. "Is this correct, beautiful? Are you uncomfortable with public displays of sex?"

"Leena, this is the owner, Master James." Lilly interrupted to make the introduction.

"Yes, Master James, I have no desire to perform sexually in front of an audience. I'm sure I wouldn't be able to be aroused."

"Fair enough, beautiful, but it does sound like an excellent challenge. Tell me, why are you aroused now?"

Shocked at his question, she sensed he could tell and was embarrassed.

"I don't know, Master James."

"Interesting. Perhaps one day we can test this limit of yours and perhaps, I will have the pleasure of finding out."

"Yes, Master James, thank you."

"Mistress Lilly, good to see you again. I enjoyed our chat and continue to enjoy your tour. Anything I can do to make your stay with us better, let me know. I will take the information you gave me into consideration and talk with my onsite Doms."

She watched the Master of the club saunter past the other scenes on his way to the elevator. Grabbing Lilly's arm, she exploded.

"You've got to get me out of here. He's the second Dom that's hit on me. This is not why I'm here, Lilly."

"I know, child, I know. I've got you're back and there's no need to worry. Besides, I'm putting feelers out for the perv who killed Addie. It may take a couple of times coming back before we get good information."

"What do you mean coming back? Those feelers are trying to feel me. There's no way in hell I'm doing a scene here."

Her head was supposed to be looking down, but she peeked at the rest of the scenes. Several men gave her stern looks as they passed by but she averted her eyes before they said anything to Lilly.

Winding around the corner, they came upon two Dom's and a male submissive. It was obvious one Dom was more experienced than the other, because he gave instructions on proper technique in using the whip. Her focus was on his skillfully built body. He wore a black wife beater shirt and skin tight black leather pants, but the thing which turned her on, was his bare feet.

Damn, the confidence he must have.

Breathless and excited, she wanted him to turn around until he finally did.

"Shit, get me out of here…now."

"This way, Baby Girl, we'll head for the other elevator. We can go back to the juice bar."

Leena stood punching the up button continuously until the door opened. She then pulled the woman in behind her.

"Who did you see? You're white as snow."

"The Dom who was teaching was Roger. I can't believe he comes here. I thought you knew I didn't want him to know we were here."

"I also told you one of my conditions was to give any information we discover back to him. He not only comes here, he is on staff here. Several of your aunt's friends and colleagues come here as Dom's or submissives.

Really, there's no way you can hide it unless you actually want to play as a sub."

"Aren't there any other dungeons free from people she knew?"

"I'm afraid not, darlin, the Goth, occult, psychic, and BDSM communities are basically interwoven here.

"God, I hope he didn't see my face. Can we just go home for now?"

"Yes, we can. I want to stop by the bar and talk for one minute to the bartender. I promise I won't be long."

Her stomach was rolling as they stepped off the elevator, heading in the direction of the bar. She stood dutifully by the blonde woman listening to her conversation. As soon as they were through, Lilly touched her shoulder and pulled up short.

"Uh oh."

She heard a familiar male voice. "Lilly, we haven't seen you here for a while. It's good to see you again." Roger stated. "And who is this with you? Leena, I believe?" He leaned against a couch with his tanned feet crossed at the ankles and arms crossed over his chest.

Her head hung low as she slowly turned around. She refused to give him eye contact and simply stared at the floor.

"Sweetness, look at me. I'd like an answer please."

"Yes, Sir," raising her eyes to his. The submissive in her definitely recognized the Dom in him. His gorgeous body stood patiently waiting for her answer. His shirt hugged his chest and was tucked into his tight leather pants at the hips.

"Lilly showed me around tonight and brought me here to see where she plays." She swallowed hard and hoped he bought her story.

Her eyes stayed fixed on his as he raked them from her head down to her stilettos. Once they'd consumed her, they shot back to her face with a wicked smile.

"Mistress Lilly, again, we're glad you're back. She's a beautiful submissive, don't you think?"

"I certainly do, Roger. We're just on our way out."

"That's too bad. Tonight was just getting interesting. I'd love to cuff this little one to a spanking bench. Maybe another time." He winked and moved over to the bartender.

Leena reached for the doorknob to the dressing room, when she heard his voice shout across the room.

"Oh and Leena? We *will* talk tomorrow."

****

Leena didn't sleep well. She thrashed back and forth in her bed, frustrated at the reoccurring dreams of men fondling her while strapped to a table. Normally, she wouldn't care but these guys kept asking her to touch them...to read their futures. Faceless hands everywhere, stroking and teasing her body, begging for her gift. No sound came from her screaming lips until she bolted straight up in her bed, waking herself. At first she didn't realize she'd been dreaming. Her shoulders heaved trying to catch her breath. She collapsed back onto her pillow, attempting to calm her frustration from the dream.

Her hand fumbled under the bedding, searching for the remote to her television. Maybe if she watched a little early morning news and weather, it would take her mind off the dreams. The glow from the screen startled her eyes and she squinted, as she surfed through the channels. She found a local news channel and left it there. Breaking News flashed across the screen in red letters and she turned the volume up. Fear coursed through her body, numbing her as she laid there and listened. There'd been another psychic murder. The body was found in another abandoned building near the Mississippi waterfront. It was the only information they were giving out.

Her cell phone went off but she didn't even look at it. The bathroom was her first order of business. She pulled on a pair of jeans and t-shirt, then pulled her hair back in a ponytail. Her mind was running on autopilot as she paced into the kitchen and poured herself a glass of orange juice. If she ignored this business, it would go away. Her heart knew better, but if she could convince her mind, she'd be okay.

A horrendous banging on the door made her jump and yell.

"Oh Lilly, really, you have to find a better way to let me know you're here."

She fumbled with the locks, jerking the door back only to find Roger leaning against the frame out of breath.

"You didn't answer your phone. They called me into the precinct on the murder, but I had to make sure it wasn't you."

He grabbed her and held her tight in his arms. His face nuzzled her hair, then her walls came tumbling down as she burst into tears. All her pent up emotions from last night at the club plus her dreams, came pouring out. When she'd calmed, he released her and took her to a chair at the table.

"I have to go in. I'll be back when we've investigated the crime scene and made out our report. I want you to stay here. The surveillance car is still outside. Will you be okay?"

"Yes, I'm fine. You go do your job."

"No you're not, baby. I'm coming back here when Bryan and I are through. Call me if you need me for anything."

Chapter Eight

An hour later, she found herself still sitting in the same spot when he left. Her mind was fixated on the second murder, while her emotions ran the gamut from fear to rage. The murderer obviously decided to focus on psychics for his point of interest and she wanted to know why.

Tired of brooding over the lack of details, she went down to the shop once again to try and put things in some sort of order. She threw herself into organizing shelves. After thirty minutes, she realized she'd no idea what she was doing. With only a tiny bit of knowledge of witchcraft, she got lost trying to put similar items together. There was no way she knew which items went with which labels, unless it was obvious like candles or crystals.

Her frustration was interrupted by a soft tapping on the front window. She looked up to see Lilly motioning for her to open the door and let her in.

She probably wants to discuss the second murder and I really would like to avoid thinking about it.

However, she decided any diversion was welcomed over her lack of knowledge of her present task. When she reached the front door, she unbolted it noticing a young woman standing behind Lilly. She was dressed in gothic clothes with the usual black hair and make-up to match.

"Hi hon, we went to the side door and didn't get a response. So I figured you were down here trying to organize inventory again. And here you are. This is Tabby, short for Tabitha. She's one of my salespersons in my shop. She's also a practicing Wiccan and wants to concentrate on that aspect of the business. I already have a girl who does all of it for me and I was hoping you could use Tabby's expertise, since your understanding of the subject is limited."

"Oh Lilly, you're an answer to my panic. Hi Tabby. Would you be willing to start right away?"

"Yeah, I guess so. Do you have another salesperson? How much are we talking about?" the girl boldly asked.

"No, there's no one else. I read the tarot cards and fortunes. I need someone out here who knows what they are doing. It would be your responsibility as long as you turn in frequent sales reports and inventory to me so I can keep a handle on everything. I can start off with minimum wage but once I get the feel of the shop's actual worth, it could increase."

"Cool. I can start now. I'll put your inventory in its proper place and make new labels for the shelves."

"Thank you. I'd love it if you would. Lilly and I are going to be over at the table in the alcove between the shelves. Just start wherever you'd like."

Before she joined Lilly at the table, she strolled to the small refrigerator behind the counter and took out two cans of soda. She handed one to Lilly and sat across from her.

"So tell me about Tabby. What kind of worker is she? How trustworthy?"

"She's very trustworthy...loyal to a fault. Showed up in my shop three years ago wanting to work and stayed. She's a very hard worker and an excellent witch and teacher. Don't be put off by her quiet nature, she's outgoing with the shoppers. Her observational skills are very effective...she sees everything."

Leena took a gulp of her soda. "I need someone who can run this part of the shop without help and she sounds perfect. That way, I can take care of the readings myself."

"Exactly. It's why I brought her to you. And if you ever want to learn Wicca, she'll be more than willing to teach you."

"You've been a great friend, Lilly, even though you made me wear the ridiculous outfit last night."

"You have to admit it got you noticed by several Doms and especially by those connected with the club. Most of them knew your aunt and a few were good friends of hers. They'll take good care of you."

"But I wasn't there to get noticed. I was there to find information I could use to find her killer, not to become someone's submissive. I've no desire to be a part of the lifestyle. I'm not submissive. I lived on the street taking care of myself for far too long to give up my will to a man," snapped Leena.

"Really? Well, good for you. So, it shouldn't really bother you to play the part, especially since you're not submissive?" goaded Lilly.

She rolled her eyes at the older woman but didn't say a word. Her cell phone vibrated and she checked the caller I.D. It was Roger. It beeped again for a text message which she opened.

'Typing up my report now. I'll be at your house in one hour. See you then.'

"Roger's going to be here in an hour. I guess I'd better go upstairs and clean up a bit," she stated out loud.

"You do know about the second murder last night, don't you?" the woman asked.

"Yes, I saw it on the news this morning and then Roger came by because I wasn't answering my phone."

"Did he share any information with you?"

"No, Lilly, he didn't know anything…just a woman was killed. He wanted to make sure it wasn't me so he stopped here on his way to the scene."

"This business has me spooked. I don't want any of my girls out alone."

"They need to be careful, Lilly, and so should you. Well, I gotta get upstairs. Can you stay with Tabby and lock up when she's through? I'll get a key made for her later."

"Sure I can. You don't worry about a thing. I'll call you later on."

Grabbing her soda, Leena pushed her chair back and headed straight for the door at the back of the store. Once through, she threw the dead bolt and locked it from her side. She took a quick shower and then sat down on the couch waiting for Roger. She'd lost her patience with the old woman's nosiness but then again, *she* was frantic for him to fill *her* in.

The silence in her apartment was deafening. Thirty minutes were left before he'd arrive so she reached to turn on the television. Then again, she chose not to because she didn't want to hear any reports by the news media. She wanted it straight from him.

Her head leaned back on the cushion and she stared at the ceiling. Her thoughts churned over the details of her aunt's murder. A loud banging roused her from them, making her jump. The peep hole in the door was at eye level and she gave it a quick glance before opening all the locks. Roger's face was solemn when she opened the door.

"By the look on your face, it must not be good." She stepped back and let him enter, then led him into the living room. Her hand motioned to the couch where she dropped and sat, waiting for him to fill her in.

****

Roger sat next to her but didn't want to share what he saw. However, he knew she wouldn't let it go until he'd told her everything.

"No, it wasn't good. I know you won't leave me alone until I've told you everything. What I tell you stays between us. You can't even share the details with Lilly. It was another fortune teller…younger than your aunt. Tied to an old bondage table, she'd been placed in another deserted building on the opposite side of the city. Just like the first, she'd been drained of her blood in the same manner."

"Why is he going after fortune tellers? And for God's sake, why is he draining them? It doesn't make sense."

"We don't know but we're now classifying him as a serial killer."

"Did he leave any clues this time or mistakes?"

"No, he was meticulous when he cleaned up. He did leave one thing behind for us and actually, it was marked to you. It's the only reason I'm giving you any information at all."

"What was it?"

"It was a tarot card dipped in the blood of the victim. Your name was painted in blood above where the card was left and before you ask, no, he had gloves on. There weren't any prints. Leena, the card laid out was the death card."

He saw a puzzled look crinkle her eyes. "Death card? Anyone who knows about tarot knows it doesn't mean death. It's more like a major change or new beginnings. Just depends on what cards are played with it."

"There's one more thing. You may have seen the victim last night at the club. She's the one there with her Dom, who was being observed by the owner of the club."

When he saw her eyes go wide and her hand come up to her mouth, he pulled her into his arms.

"No," she pushed away from him and sat back. "What about her Dom? Does he know anything? Has he got an alibi?"

"Hey, hold on. That's enough…no more information. No more speculation."

"I want to see the crime scene, Roger. I might be able to touch something and get a vision. I can help you. Let me help so we can shut this guy down."

"We? I don't think so, Sweetness. And speaking of we, what was your reason to be at the club again? Lilly wanted to show you or you wanted her to help you do your own investigation? I'm not stupid, Leena. You need to stop before something happens to you."

"I never thought you were, but I can't sit back and do nothing. My gift can help you. Use me, please."

Oh, how I wish you'd let me use you.

"As tempting as it sounds and as hot as you looked last night, I'm afraid it wouldn't be wise. You made quite a stir with several Doms last night. There seems to be a line formed hoping you'll return and be their submissive for the evening. I'm included on the list, by the way."

"Why does everyone consider me submissive? I'm not. Lilly insisted I be one last night. I wasn't comfortable with it."

"What makes you think you're not?" He sat smirking at her.

"I spent most of my teens living on the streets and traveling with my mom's family. I took care of myself. I answered to no one…no man. I didn't then and I don't intend to now."

He watched her stand and pace in front of the television. He knew he hit a nerve somewhere deep inside when he saw her jaw clench. Her frustration level was rising.

"You seem to have a problem with men?" He stood moving slowly toward her.

"Yeah, I have a problem with dominating men who bully and verbally abuse women. One who makes them believe they're nothing. I lived that way until I left home. I don't need to again."

She turned to go into the kitchen when he suddenly shoved her against the wall with his body. He moved her hair over to the side and brushed his lips up to her ear. They stood still for a few minutes, and she didn't fight him.

"Your heart is racing, Leena. Is it fear or does this excite you?" His fingers stroked over her arm as her skin pebbled under his touch. His body pressed further into her, licking his way from her ear to the back of her neck.

"Is this what you *don't* want, baby? A man controlling your body, making you feel what you *don't* want to feel, and having your body tell you otherwise?" He placed a kiss on the back of her neck and a small whimper escaped her throat.

"Does this make you burn?" Another kiss was placed to the side, just under her ear.

"Listen to your heart beat. Your breathing is getting faster. Does this turn you on, lover? Do I make you hot?"

He sucked on her earlobe breathing into it.

"The things I want to do to you. Make you beg me to stroke you, caress your body, and plunge myself deep inside you. Is this what you're afraid of, Leena?"

She threw her head back against him, whispering into the air.

"Yes, oh God, yes. Please, Roger."

He picked her up and carried her into her bedroom, laying her on the bed. His eyes stayed glued to her face while she watched him slowly slip her shirt over her head, tossing it on the floor. Lifting her up in a sitting position, he gently reached behind and unhooked her bra. The straps slipped off her shoulders easily, letting her soft perky breasts fall out of the cups.

"Beautiful," he breathed and took a nipple into his mouth, tenderly sucking. She moaned, touching his hair and pulling his head closer.

Laying her back on the pillow, he gently brushed his fingertips between her breasts, down to the top of her jeans. While he skillfully unbuttoned each one, he smiled when she raised her hips, making it easier to remove them.

Chapter Nine

Leena watched Roger stand, removing his clothes. His body was gorgeous in a quiet kind of way. There was no huge six pack, only tanned, smooth skin stretched tightly over his muscles. She never guessed that underneath his suit was a man with incredible definition in all the right places. His cock was erect, bobbing as he approached her.

"Are you afraid of me, Leena? I'm a Dom, and you just buckled under my control. Your desire has already filled the room, baby, so you can't deny your feelings."

She stared hard at his face, thinking over his words and comparing them to her reactions. He'd definitely made her cave to his will and all she wanted to do was please him. It was not her normal nature and it frightened her.

"Yeah, Roger, I'm a bit afraid of you. No one but my father has ever made me succumb to their will."

He crawled up on the bed, moving slowly over her and laying his hips across her thighs. His cock pressed into her stomach, twitching as his erection continued to grow. Her eyes studied him, reaching up and stroking her fingers in his hair. "I find myself uncharacteristically wanting to please you and it terrifies me."

"What exactly terrifies you?" He threaded his legs under hers and wrapped his arms over and under her torso. With one swift move, he held her tight and flipped them both over, with him on the bottom and her stretched out on top of him.

Her hands grabbed his shoulders, steadying herself from the sudden movement. Again, she felt his cock twitch and press into her. The look on his face told her he expected her to answer. She licked her lips and smiled.

"I'm scared of getting lost in you. I'm terrified of not having control over my own life. You'd be so easy to fall for."

"Well, we'll just have to keep it from happening, won't we?"

His breath trailed from her ear over to her lips. He placed small, brief kisses on her mouth, teasing her. She wanted more from him and proceeded to force his head down. He resisted the pull of her hands, smiling at her. If she didn't know better, he'd read her mind.

"What is it you want, Miss Price?"

Her mind took control telling her two could play at this game of seduction. Placing her hands on his chest, she pushed herself up enough to move her hips above his. Her slit was wet and his cock slid perfectly in between the lips of her pussy.

Right where I want him.

Then she lowered her weight and rested on his cock. "Mr. Black," sliding her pussy lips forward and stopping. "What makes you think I want anything from you?" She slid back on his cock to her original position.

Her eyes raked over his face, noticing his eyes were closed and his head was pushing back into the pillow.

"Oh fuck, Miss Price. You feel so good."

She continued to slide his cock between her lips, until he moved low enough to align the head to her entrance. Both of them gasped when he plunged deep inside and gripped her hips.

"Ride me, Leena. Let me feel your body ride me."

She didn't need any more encouragement from him. Her hips rotated in circles, grinding against his crotch, as his fingers dug into her ass. She pulled her hips up almost to the tip of his cock, letting her hands keep her balanced.

His hands then pulled her hips down, slamming against his crotch. Again, they both gasped.

"What are you doing to me, Roger?"

"The same thing you're doing to me."

Her desire built until her body couldn't hold back any longer, releasing all of her passion, and plunging her pussy up and down on his cock.

"God, Roger, I'm cumming. Yes...baby, oh yes."

"Give it to me, woman, fuck me hard."

Clamping her fingers onto his chest, she almost pulled the patch of dark hair out. Her orgasm was a long one, clenching through each wave of pleasure. When the last wave hit her body, she shuddered and then went rigid, collapsing on top of him. She fought to catch her breath while listening to his heart beat. She could feel his hands softly massaging her back and ass. His fingers felt wonderful, and made her relaxed and groggy.

Suddenly, she jerked her head off his chest, studying his face. She'd no idea whether Roger had made it or not. His eyes were closed, off in his own world, while he continued to stroke her back and butt.

Wide eyed, she apologized, "Roger, oh my God, did you cum? I'm so sorry."

Laughing at her, he pulled her hair back in a ponytail and answered. "Yes, baby, I came and it was good. I think yours was better and it made me hot."

"I got so lost in mine, I wasn't paying attention to you."

"Then I did my job effectively, I'd say."

She laid her head against his chest again. "Oh, hell yeah, you did."

His continued back rub lulled her into a deep sleep, as she drifted off satisfied.

Sometime in the early morning, she jerked awake with him wrapped around her. Carefully, she wiggled and pushed until her body worked free from his. She picked up her jeans from the floor and tiptoed into the bathroom closing the door behind her. Her blue nightshirt hung on the back of the door. She grabbed it, throwing it on over her head. Sitting on the toilet, she relieved herself and then slipped on her jeans.

The other bathroom door opened into her aunt's bedroom. She walked through, into the hall, and finally stopped in the kitchen, grabbing a can of soda from the refrigerator. Then she went back into her aunt's room, opened the patio door, and stepped out to the table and chairs. It was still dark outside, but the street was lit up with a few people roaming around. Seemed the French Quarter was always busy, no matter what time of day.

Her thoughts went to the conversation and events from last night. She never did get him to give a definite answer about letting her look at the crime scene. He managed to shift the topic to the club and she needed to ask him again before he left for work.

What in the hell did I let happen last night? What was I thinking? She wondered.

"You weren't, Leena," she mumbled as she took a sip of her soda.

I could've stopped him. Why didn't I?

The soda bubbled in her mouth as she took another drink from the can. "Because you didn't want him to stop." Aggravated with herself, she slammed the can down on the table, popping some of the soda into the air.

"You didn't want me to stop what, baby?"

Leena jumped hearing him speak behind her. "Oh my God, Roger. You scared me. I didn't hear you open the door."

"You were obviously deep in thought. Were you having a conversation with yourself?" He sat in a chair next to her.

"Yeah, I was. I remembered you never gave me a definitive answer about visiting the crime scene. I need to see it."

"I'll take you tonight. They should be through processing everything. This is the last, Leena. No more, so don't even ask me should any more occur, which I pray they don't. Now answer my original question."

She knew exactly what he referred to. Taking another sip, she cleared her throat and answered.

"I should've stopped you last night. We can't go that far again. I don't want a love relationship, Roger. You've become a great friend and I want to keep it…but not with benefits."

"So you're telling me you didn't enjoy what happened between us?"

Leena stared hard into his eyes and couldn't tell what he was thinking. His voice turned stoic, sounding a bit like an interrogator.

"No, I didn't say that. Yes, I enjoyed it…too much. But I need a friend right now, not a lover. I don't want to be a couple." She lied through her teeth and it broke her heart, watching him turn cold in front of her eyes.

He didn't answer, simply continued to scrutinize her face. After several minutes, he stood. "I'm going to go home and change for work. I'll pick you up this evening around seven. Is the time good for you?"

"Yes, that's fine. I'll be in the store so you won't have to come up the back way. Roger, please, I'm sorry."

"See you then. I'll let myself out so don't forget to lock up behind me."

Fuck! I blew that...now he's hurt and angry. Damn, why do I have to care? I can't let myself like him.

His footsteps sounded on the wooden stairs at the side of the building. She stood, went to the door, and locked all of the locks. Disgusted with herself, she turned, going into the bathroom to shower before going downstairs. She mentally kicked herself because she hurt Roger.

How am I going to fix this? I've got to come up with something before tonight.

By the time she'd showered, fixed her hair, and dressed, the sun had crested over the horizon, illuminating the French Quarter. She made her way downstairs, swinging by the fridge for orange juice on the way. The sun peeked through the windows, lighting up the entire store. She looked around thinking things were different, flipping on the lights for a better view. The shelves were organized, labeled, and clean. Tabby had done an excellent job making the store ready for business.

There's no way I could've done this job. She'll be an excellent employee.

Leena went into her small room behind the counter to check for things she would need to begin giving readings. She'd already brought her personal crystals and tarot cards, placing them on the table. There were three chairs in the room. Two were placed at the table and one was placed at the side, off in a corner. A black altar cloth was draped across the table giving a dark background to her brilliantly colored cards.

Perfect.

The crystals were in a small pile and she arranged a few on the table. The rest of them, she scattered around the room to give off positive vibes. Her mind was made up. She would open for business tomorrow, realizing her job might be slow until people became familiar and comfortable with her. However, the tourists wouldn't know the difference.

The sound of a key turning in the lock of the front door, roused her from her planning. She stepped down the two steps from the room to behind the counter in time to see Tabby relock the front door. Her eyes watched the girl survey the room, holding her hands in front of her body, and mouthing words she couldn't hear.

When the girl's eyes spotted Leena standing at the front, she jerked her hands to her sides.

"I'm sorry, I didn't mean to startle you. What were you doing just now?"

"I was blessing the store and warding off any evil presence."

"Good. I like that. You've done a wonderful job with the inventory, Tabby. It looks great in here. I'm grateful for your help."

"Thank you, Miss Leena. I came in for a few odd things I didn't get done yesterday, and of course, to bless the place. You can't be too careful."

"Well, tomorrow we'll open for business. Readings probably won't be much, so I'll help out here as best as I can. I can at least ring up the merchandise."

"You may be busier than you think. You never know what the tourists will do."

"I need to clear my head a bit so I'm going to walk to Jackson Square and look around. I'm not sure how long I'll be gone, but I've got to be back by seven."

"Are you going by yourself?"

"Yes. I'll be fine. I know exactly how to get there and back."

"Wait a minute." She saw the girl go over to the counter and pull a necklace off a display. When she strode back to her, she witnessed a small red, cloth pouch tied with a white string, and suspended on a thin piece of leather which was knotted together at both ends. Leena ducked her head as the girl draped the leather over Leena's head. "Here, wear this under your top, against your skin. I made a few up fresh yesterday, hoping we'd be opening soon."

"What is this?"

"It's a mojo bag. It's made to protect the wearer from harm or evil. Just trust me and don't take it off."

"I won't...I promise." Her hand patted the pockets of her jeans, making sure her keys were there. Her money was rolled and placed in the other pocket. She pulled her sunglasses from the top of her head down to her nose, and pushed them back on her face. Walking out the front door, she waved goodbye to Tabby, headed down the small street to Royal Street. There, she would find St. Peter Street and take a straight shot to Jackson Square. Actually, she intended to go straight to Decatur Street to the Café Du Monde for breakfast. Then she would make her way back through the Square.

Chapter Ten

It felt good to sit in the open air café and watch people going up and down the street. Horse drawn carriages were lining up, waiting for customers wanting a tour. The beignet melted in her mouth. It was surprising how many were already eating at the café, but then this place was open all day and night. Families, people heading into work, street performers, and artists all stopped by to share breakfast. Too many people were crowded together here, and she needed to think to sort things out. She'd head to the Square, grab a bench underneath the trees, and form a plan.

Briskly walking across the street, she entered through the gates, found an empty bench in the shade, and sat. Andrew Jackson's statue was in full view from where she sat. Also, she had a great view of the Saint Louis Cathedral. Her bench was off the main sidewalk so hopefully, she'd have plenty of semi-privacy.

It was muggy outside, but at least she wasn't in the direct sunlight. She leaned back on the bench, enjoying the small breeze periodically blowing through. Her eyes studied the church and she had to admit it was very beautiful. Thinking of her father's church, she wondered if the same kind of people worshiped in the Cathedral.

Aggravated, she refused to think of her father, making herself watch the people walking through the Square instead. Her eyes studied each male walking alone, seeing if she could get a feel for the killer. Was he a loner, did he sit in places like this to pick his victims?

This is getting me nowhere. I know what I have to do. I need to explain to Roger why I'm not ready to be seriously involved with anyone, but I care for him. Now is just not the time to let him distract me.

She stood, walking out the gate and around to the St. Ann Street side. Artists were displaying their paintings against the fence for people to browse through. They were amazing and very talented, young and old alike.

If she had the money, she'd have bought a painting of an old sea captain standing on a cliff overlooking the ocean. The colors were vibrant and the look on his face haunted her. The artist was a young man, who truly wanted her to have it, but needed to get out of it what he put into it. She thought for a moment about her inheritance, wanting to take the money from the account. Her inner disciplinarian reminded her she'd promised herself not to touch the money except for the shop. Leena determined she simply couldn't afford it, and it wouldn't be fair to ask him to hold it for two to three months. Regretfully, she said no and strolled on.

A few more pictures caught her eyes as she slowly strolled down the sidewalk, but nothing like the sea captain. Rounding the corner into the wide street in front of the Cathedral, her face broke into a broad smile at the variety of talent displayed. Musicians, jugglers, fortune tellers, mimes, caricature artists doing live work…so many talented people were there to delight her senses. Crafts from wind chimes to glass sun catchers and belts were available for purchase.

Leena had slowly made her way across three quarters of the displays, when she looked up at the clock on the Cathedral, realizing she needed to start for home. Roger would pick her up at seven and she needed time to shower and change. Focused on St. Peter Street, she threaded her way through the throngs of people which had filled the street.

I didn't realize how much the crowd down here had grown. There are people everywhere.

Once she cleared the immediate rush, she paced to St. Peter Street and found she battled against more crowds on the way out of Jackson Square.

God, I hate crowds. This is like swimming against the current. I need to find a less traveled cross street and go over a block.

She did exactly what she'd set out to do, taking a deep breath of relief. Her eyes were tempted by the shops along the block…so many cool things to see.

When my shop gets settled, I'm coming back here to shop. These are wonderful.

The end of the block was ahead, aware she needed to make a left turn, she wasn't able to make it. Out of nowhere, a huge group of people came at her. Once again, she fought against bodies pushing against her. Disoriented, panic set in.

Finally, they passed her and she found herself on a darkened street. Small raindrops were falling and getting heavier by the minute. She continued down the street, noticing men were standing in the doorways of several shops, staring hard at her as she passed. Fast footsteps sounded close behind her. She turned but no one was there. The street was totally deserted.

Where did all the crowds go?

Her pace quickened, trying to get to the corner as soon as she could but it never came. Only a long row of shops on a deserted street. Again, she heard footsteps behind her, so instead of turning around, she ducked into a shop. The people in the shop stared, showing no emotion or asking if they could help her. It was a Voodoo/Hoodoo shop catering to authentic followers and not tourists. A tall, slender woman stood behind the counter eyeing her. Immediately, she stepped outside and crossed the street. By this time, her sense of direction was totally turned around, and her emotions were off the charts.

Shit, girl, you lived on the streets for years, what's the matter with you?

An opportunity to turn and get off the street she currently was on, opened up and she took it, except she turned right. There were a couple of shops but they were closed. She continued to walk down the street and found herself in a residential cul-de-sac.

Okay, I'm really lost now.

As she turned to back track her steps, a man turned onto the street headed straight toward her. When she stepped to the side in order to walk to the side once they reached each other, he moved directly into her path. They danced like this several times before Leena started to run back to find a house for help.

The man kept coming toward her, forcing her into a hedge. Reaching her, he placed his hand on her shoulder and tipped his hat up.

"Leena Price, is that you? Are you okay?"

Through heavy tears, she saw it was her aunt's lawyer.

"No, Mr. Stevenson, I'm not. I'm lost and I think someone was following me. I need to get home."

"You're in the opposite direction of your home. Not to worry, though, I'll get you home safe and sound. And please, Leena, won't you call me Bradly?" He extended his hand to her and gently spoke. "Come, I'll take you home now."

He pulled her arm through his as they strolled to the corner where he hailed a taxi.

"We'll take the fastest way home. I've got a feeling you're not up for a long walk right now."

His hand reached for the door, opening it, and helping her into the back of the cab. She scooted to the opposite side, giving him room to sit, while he gave the driver the address to her shop.

She looked at him in surprise, questioning his ability to quickly rattle it off.

"As many times as I've dictated the address on legal documents, young lady, I know it like my own."

"Oh, it surprised me, is all. It's fine. I must admit my brain is mush. What were you doing down at the Square today?"

"When I'm lucky enough to get time off from work, I often walk down there. There was a band playing this afternoon I wanted to hear. I thought I saw you walking around and then leaving the Square. I attempted to catch up with you but then you took a turn in the opposite direction into a not so safe neighborhood. You're a quick walker, Leena. I almost didn't find you on the back street. You took so many turns, it was hard to find you again. I'm afraid I'm probably the one you felt following you…I'm sorry."

Her smile felt fake as she tried to accept his apology. "I'm just glad you found me."

The driver pulled up in front of Addie's Mojo and stopped. She reached into her jeans, searching for a twenty dollar bill, but Bradly put his hand on hers.

"No. I've got this, besides, I'm going back to the office, so I'll take the taxi there. Just promise you'll have dinner with me some evening soon."

"Um, okay. I'll call your office when I'm available. Thank you, Bradly."

"Is this your way of saying don't call me, I'll call you, Miss Price?"

"No. I don't play that particular game. Thank you again."

She'd pulled her keys out of her other pocket, unlocked the shop door, and walked into a pristine store ready to open for business in the morning. Her lungs filled with fresh, safe, and calm air. She was home.

Tabby is an angel. I need to raise her pay as soon as I know I can afford it.

Exhaustion hit her as she climbed the stairs to the apartment. She had an hour before Roger would arrive which was barely enough time for a shower.

Well, crap, no nap for me.

****

Roger had no clue how tonight would go. Leena's frankness hurt more than he thought it would. He wasn't able to keep the cold out of his tone when he told her goodbye. He hated it but he couldn't pretend it didn't bother him.

The sex had been intensely satisfying and the idea it wasn't happening again saddened him. Not just because of the sex itself, but because he had feelings for her. More than he wanted to admit.

Bryan is right…I'm falling for her. And she just put a halt to it.

His tires squealed as his car whipped into a parking space in front of the store. She locked the door behind her just as he got out of his car.

"Wow, you're ready. I timed it just right."

"You said seven, didn't you? It's seven now." She sounded hateful and he winced.

"Leena, I'm…"

"No. Roger, please. I'm sorry…I didn't mean it to be hateful. I'm simply nervous and I had a horrible afternoon."

"What happened this afternoon?"

"Later…after we see the crime scene. We'll talk and I'll even buy the first round."

"Okay, deal." He opened her door, watching her slide in and buckle her seat belt. Sliding behind the steering wheel, he threw the car into reverse, backed out, and then put it in drive, taking off like a bat out of hell.

"This abandoned warehouse is a bit further than the first. You'll have to put up with my charm till we get there. Look in the box at your feet and pull out whatever music you want. Or we can load my MP3 player and you can scroll through it."

He smiled as she continued to browse his numerous playlists. She settled on his Doobie Brothers playlist and smiled, melting his insides.

"That's one of my favorites," he said.

They sang each of the songs until they reached a neighborhood of broken down, empty buildings. He drove to the end of one block and parked across the drive, blocking the garage door entrance. The doors were missing and many windows were broken out.

"This one wasn't even closed up. Why didn't anyone hear it and report it while it was going on?"

"Come on, I'll show you."

"Is her body still here?" He saw her eyes were big as saucers, probably from fear he thought.

"No, I'll walk you through what we found. Come follow me. You'll have to take my hand because there are no bulbs in the lights. They were destroyed, we're guessing, after he finished. This was done at night so he had to have light. Unless he brought his own and a generator."

Chapter Eleven

Leena slid her hand in Roger's, following carefully behind him. Even though it was evening, it was still light outside. However, across the building from the garage doors, it was extremely dark.

When she stepped across the threshold, a chill crept deep into her joints and body. Pure evil had been in the room. She felt it everywhere...her body jerked back from the emotions.

"What's wrong, Leena? We need to cross to the far wall where the crime scene actually took place."

"I'm coming...just overwhelmed by the amount of malevolence present in this place. Something terrible happened in here and the building is filled with it. Go slow so I can keep breathing."

"Huh?"

"I'll explain later...just keep going."

She squeezed his hand, matching his footsteps step for step. Suddenly, her body smacked into him when he abruptly stopped.

"What's wrong?" she questioned.

"I ran into a generator the investigators used to operate their lights. Hang on while I try to fire it up. It doesn't give off much light, but at least we'll be able to see a little bit."

Once the generator was running, Leena saw the light was directed toward what appeared to be an exam table. In fact, it was exactly that, a doctor's exam table.

"Oh my God."

"I know, Leena…trust me, I know. Before I give you Bryan's and my opinion, do you think you'd be able to touch the table?"

"I'll try, but if I start convulsing, pull me out of here."

Letting go of his hand, she inched to the table, and hesitated before placing her hands on the stirrups left in the open position. Malicious vibes were strongest here, and frankly, she didn't want to touch the table at all.

Her hands grabbed hold of the stirrups, her body jerking back at the touch. Immediately, she stood in the room, watching the young woman's naked body being touched by four hands. She couldn't see the face or bodies attached to the hands, but knew they were both male. The stronger presence enjoyed teasing the woman's body, constantly stroking and pinching but never touching the most sensual areas.

The woman's feet were placed and tied to the stirrups. She raised her eyes to the woman's face again, searching her eyes. They appeared glassy to her, as if she'd been drugged.

It's the reason she didn't fight him.

Next thing she knew, his body was between her thighs, as his hands spread her knees apart wide. From where she stood, she could only see his hands on her knees, while his hips moved.

"Oh my God, I'm not sure, but I think he raped her," she heard herself scream. For a brief moment, she could feel his emotions. Cold, sadistic feelings ran through her mind similar to tendrils snaking through her blood. Just before Leena thought he would orgasm, the violence of his emotions knocked her back against Roger, releasing the stirrups.

"What did you see, Leena?"

"Something horrible, Roger. This was so close to the dream I had the other night. I was tied to a table while hands from out of the darkness, stroked over my body. Two sets of hands were in this room torturing the woman. The woman was drugged, Roger. She couldn't fight or scream.

It's no wonder not one person reported hearing it. And I think he raped her before he killed her, but I didn't see it happen. I felt his emotions. He's foul and wicked…takes great pleasure when he tortures his victims. His emotions threw me off. I didn't see him kill her."

"She was murdered just like your Aunt was… exsanguination. Let's get out of here. Can we go somewhere for coffee or drinks and talk?"

"I've got a better idea. We'll go back to my apartment and talk. I can fix coffee, if that's what you want or I have beer. I need to come down from this where it's quiet."

"Beer will work."

The ride back was completely silent. Rather than focus on the details of her vision, she fretted over how she'd explain her reaction to Roger from the night before. Once they arrived, they climbed the stairs at the side of the apartment. It's a good thing she didn't throw all of the deadbolts and extra locks when they left the shop.

"You want coffee or beer?" as she sauntered over to the refrigerator.

Roger sat at the table and answered, "Beer, please."

"Me too. I need it and it'll save me from having to brew a whole pot for one person."

Grabbing two bottles from the fridge, she handed him one, then sat down across from him. She took a huge swig from the bottle and slammed it down in front of her.

"Look, Roger, before we discuss the crime and what I saw, I need to explain my behavior last night."

"You don't need to explain anything. You made yourself very clear."

"No, I didn't. I fucked it up because I was scared." He raised his hand and she continued. "Don't interrupt and let me talk. I came here looking to start a new life with my Aunt…to reconnect with family who loved me. I woke up one morning to find my dream would never come true. I wasn't looking for romance or a hook up because I fuck up relationships. I've got trust issues."

She stopped, chugged another drink, catching her breath.

"Then here you came with all your sexual good looks and wanted to be protective. No one but my Nana had ever done that. Well, not the sexual part…just protective. I'll be honest. I care about you, I do. Much more than I want to. Last night was, well, I can't put it into words. What I'm trying to say is, I can't afford to build a relationship, other than friendship, with you now. I want to help find her killer and a romance would keep both of us from focusing. Yes, I pushed you away but it wasn't a rejection. If I hurt you, please forgive me."

Nervously, she picked up her beer again, drinking the rest. It was a long time before he spoke to her. She feared he would leave.

Finally, he smiled. "I accept your apology and explanation. Know this, I'm not going anywhere and when this business is over, we'll talk again."

Her eyes were wide, blinking at his response. His head fell back and he laughed out loud. At a loss how to take him, she ducked her head and softly answered.

"Fair enough."

"Now, let's go over the details of your vision. You said you saw two pair of hands; could you pick up anything about them other than they were both male?" He pulled his cell phone from his pocket as she watched him begin to take notes.

"Well, the hands were stroking the woman but not with a sensual feel. They were rough and pinching her skin.

I can't even begin to quantify the evil I felt watching them. One male had a weaker personality than the other. It felt to me, he played the part of a gopher or servant. The other male was the stronger one, controlling everything. He's definitely the same one who killed my aunt and he delights in the pain he gives his victims. The torture he gives is a sexual stimulant for him. And he has no remorse."

"A sociopath…pure and simple." Roger continued to make notes on his phone as she sat and watched.

He's very thorough and conscientious. It'll be worth it to work together.

"You said her eyes had a glassy appearance?"

"Yes, I know he drugged her. She didn't react to anything he did to her, no noises or movement at all. And her eyes were open."

"Probably the date rape drug. Since we don't have blood or probably even urine, we can take samples of her hair. The hair is viable up to a month. I'll make sure it's done. So…he raped her? We'll test for fluids left behind but I can almost promise you he wore a condom. He's too smart not to cover all of his tracks."

"I don't know. I really didn't look closely. The scene turned my stomach when I saw her poor eyes."

"What Bryan and I know is the cause of death is exsanguination. Her arms were draped over the side of the table so the blood would drain by gravity into whatever they collected it in. Tubing was again placed in her jugular veins and filled a container. They propped the head of the table in order for gravity to pull her blood into the tubing. There were no prints, no clues…it was cleaned spotless. Only the Death card was left behind with your name over it."

"As I said before, it doesn't mean death, only a big change or event is going to happen. The killer obviously knows nothing about Tarot."

"Anything else you can think of?"

"No. Roger, I want to help you catch this guy. Please don't shut me out."

****

Roger sat with his elbow propped on the table with his chin resting on his fist. He stared hard into her eyes, trying to imagine how her mind worked. His lungs filled with a deep breath of air which he slowly let out. Sitting back in his chair, he ran his fingers through his hair and shrugged.

"As long as you do things my way, Leena, I won't shut you out. There'll be no more snooping around with Lilly. She needs to be aware that she and her girls are at great risk. If you go back to the club, I'll accompany you. Is that clear?"

"Very clear." His gaze held hers in an accusing stare. She squirmed in her chair, reinforcing his knowledge of the effect he had on her. A smile played across his lips.

"What?"

"What do you mean what?" He knew exactly what he was doing.

"You're doing that smiling thing."

"Smiling thing? I don't know what you mean."

"Never mind. I'm too tired to argue…need sleep."

"I'd better go and let you sleep. I need to go in early to go over what you've told me with Bryan."

"Yeah, we're opening for business tomorrow and I need to have my smarts functioning."

"Well, congrats on the big day. Thank you, Leena. I know this thing you do takes a lot out of you, but you're a big help to us. Even though some don't believe, I do."

"Are you talking about Bryan?"

"He's coming around but yeah, he's one of them. Okay, I'm out of here. I'll come by tomorrow sometime and peek in on you. Come throw the locks."

She laughed for the first time this evening, the sound making his cock hard. He wished they'd met under different circumstances.

Maybe one day, she'll open up to me.

"See you tomorrow, Sweet Girl."

He leaned down and kissed her forehead.

"Night, Roger."

He stood on the landing until he heard all the locks click into place, then turned and descended the stairs. This woman had him tied up in knots to the point his focus was off. Maybe she's right in her determination to avoid personal relationships. No matter what she wanted, he intended to stay close.

The best bet for investigating now would be the club. There's definitely a BDSM influence. Hopefully, someone will pick up on something. The fetish community may be large but the grapevine is wide open among them. She can be my sub…I can protect her. This way, Lilly won't have to be involved.

Figuring he'd formed a good plan, he looked at his watch, realized it was late, and started the engine. It was a twenty minute drive back to his apartment, maybe less since there weren't many on the streets tonight. Hopefully, his arrival wouldn't wake the Tascals up. It was only two hours until they would be up baking breads and pastries for the day. Papa Tascal was a bear when he didn't get enough sleep. Of course, if he told them it was because of a girl, their whole temperament would change.

Chapter Twelve

The alarm blared loudly, startling Leena from her deep sleep. She slapped the button off, slowly crawling out from under the sheet. After a quick shower, she felt almost human again. Searching through her closet, she found the multi-colored broomstick shirt her aunt had hung the night she arrived. A tear slid down her cheek, remembering the woman who fiercely loved her. She grabbed a white peasant blouse to complete the look expected of her.

Normally, she wore very little makeup due to the natural coloring of her skin and eyes. However, keeping with the popularity and tradition of fortune tellers, she chose to wear charcoal shadow, black mascara, and heavy Kohl black liner. Once she became established with her own regulars, she'd be herself and not push the hype.

On the bureau was a small wooden chest containing various rings, bracelets, necklaces, and earrings. She chose several rings and bracelets to put on both hands and wrists. Brushing her long dark hair down and back from her face, she elected not to wear a scarf around her head. She fastened huge silver hoop earrings in her ears, looked in the mirror, and was pleased with the result.

Beaded sandals would be the perfect complement to her outfit and she slipped them onto her feet. Satisfied with herself, she strolled to the fridge, poured herself a glass of juice, and headed for the inside stairwell.

When she went into the shop, the lights were already on, and Tabby was walking throughout the shop carrying what appeared to be a strange looking plant, smoking in her hands.

What on earth?

She caught Tabby's attention and the young woman looked over at her smiling.

"Good morning, Miss Leena. I'm burning sage to clear the shop of negative vibes before I bless it."

"Do you always do this where you're working?"

"Actually no, word on the street is there's someone out there killing fortune tellers. I figure we can use all the positive vibes we can get."

"Great idea." Leena went behind the counter and stood, watching the young woman while she went through her blessing ritual. She dressed in solid black, matching her makeup and hair. A silver stud stuck through her bottom lip, painted with black lip gloss, and a diamond stud glistened on her nose. She smile to herself. *She's perfect.*

"All done. You ready to get started?"

Leena looked at the clock above the door…nine o'clock straight up.

"Let's start this party, Tabby. Go ahead, unlock the door, and turn on the neon open sign."

The younger woman busied herself with straightening shelves and making sure everything was well stocked. Leena smiled, knowing everything was in order simply because she's seen the girl work hard the week before. Confident the store was in excellent hands, she turned, marched through the door into her psychic sanctuary.

The table was laid out as she'd left it, so she sat down and picked up her deck of cards. Her hands closed around the deck, almost in a loving caress, taking deep breaths in and out. She cleared her mind of all interfering thoughts, shuffling the cards as she did. Once satisfied, she placed the bottom third of the deck in a pile on the table. Then, she separated the middle third, placing it to the left of the third pile. The remaining third was placed to the left of the second pile.

Focused solely on the cards, she picked up the piles in the order she laid them down. Again, she lovingly held the deck in her hands, deep in thought.

"I'm seeking an answer to my question and thanking the Universe in advance for its answer. Will the re-opening of Addie's Mojo be successful?"

After a few more moments of meditation, she slid the top card of the deck, laying it face up on the table. Card number two was placed face up to the left of the first card. Finally, the third card from the top of the deck was placed to the left of the second in the same manner. The rest of the deck was set across the table, away from the three cards.

Before studying the cards, she spoke her request once more, calming her spirit with slow breaths. Her eyes opened, studying each card from right to left. The first card was The Sun…such an excellent start.

It's in the first position, too.

Next, was The Ace of Pentacles. Again, it was a very good card. Her smile broke into a frown when the third card came into her line of vision. The Moon, in all its dimly lit glory, confused her celebration of the first two cards.

What was the Universe trying to tell her?

Startled by Tabby poking her head in through the curtain of beads, she yelled, slamming her hand onto her chest.

"I'm sorry. I didn't mean the scare you. I wanted to make sure you're okay. We don't have any customers yet, but it still early."

"It's okay. I was lost in thought and you just surprised me."

"What're you doing?"

"Oh, I just did a reading for myself asking about the shop."

"Cool. What did the cards say? I don't know Tarot but I want to eventually learn."

"Well, here let me show you. The first card is The Sun and it's the most positive card in the entire deck. Its light illuminates everything, bringing warmth, energy, and growth. It basically means happiness, health, good marriage, and success."

"Awesome."

"The second card is the Ace of Pentacles or Ace of Coins. It symbolizes prosperity, stability, and success. I was excited with the reading until I got to the third card. The Moon is not a very positive or encouraging card as the other two. Look at the picture on it. The colors are dark and the moon's light is dim, casting shadows all around. There are dogs howling at the moon and a crayfish crawling from the water. The moon has an effect on all life forms and a pull on the tides of the ocean. The meaning of the card is uncertainty, illusion, and emotional instability. It's more of a warning to proceed with caution and not jumping directly into things. Basically, it's a mystery."

"It sounds confusing."

Just then, the bell attached to the front door sounded.

"I think that's my cue," Tabby announced.

Leena cleared the cards for the next reading in case she should have a client today who wanted one. Placing the deck back on the table, she stepped down into the shop, hoping she could help Tabby in some manner.

The rest of the morning went very well. Tourists were out in droves and stopped in to see what the shop sold. The sales were great and Leena spent her time behind the cash register, ringing up the purchases. She'd actually forgotten about her own card reading and experienced a successful outlook.

Several of her aunt's regular customers came in to purchase their Wicca supplies. They were pleasant and became very friendly, once they realized who her aunt was. A few of them shared stories of her aunt, making her laugh and smile. Her heart was happy and on Cloud Nine.

Around noon, the amount of customers slowed down. Most of the tourists were stopping in at their favorite restaurant for lunch. She had Tabby call a place for takeout and had it delivered for the two of them.

While they were waiting for the delivery, a man ambled into the shop carrying a huge package asking for Leena. It was the painter who she'd admired his work from the day before. When he recognized her, a huge smile spread across his face.

"It's you, marvelous. You, young lady, have a very generous admirer. This was purchased this morning for you and I was told to immediately deliver it. I must admit, I was paid quite a lot for it as well. I hope you enjoy it, Miss."

With that, he set the package at her feet, leaning it against a shelf, and turned on his heel, leaving the shop.

She stood speechless. Who on earth would have bought her a gift? Roger. It has to be Roger. He knows better.

"Well, come on. Open it. I want to see what someone sent you," urged Tabby.

She went ripping through the paper it was wrapped in, spouting several 'Oh mys' as she did. When the paper was completely ripped away, Leena stood back in total disbelief.

"It's the Sea Captain. I don't believe it. Who could have done this? Oh, my God, who was watching me?"

Lilly entered the shop just as the artist, who delivered the package, left.

"How beautiful, you bought a painting. It's mysterious and haunting. The sea captain's eyes seem to see straight through you, and the colors of the cliffs and ocean are so vibrant. I'd almost swear it was a photograph."

Tabitha turned, strolling over to help another customer. Leena held the canvas up in front of her eyes, perusing every inch.

"It really does, doesn't it? I fell in love with it the minute I saw it. Something about the captain calls to me. Of course, I couldn't afford it at the time."

"Already spending your inheritance, huh?" the older woman teased with a twinkle in her eyes.

"No I didn't buy it. My aunt's money is strictly for the shop. You weren't here, were you? The artist himself brought this no more than ten minutes ago. He said it was a gift from a man who'd seen me admiring it yesterday. He talked with the artist after I left, buying it as a gift for me.

He ordered it to be delivered in person but the purchaser was to be kept anonymous."

"Where on earth are you going to put it?"

"Not sure yet...I'll have it framed first and then take it from there."

Roger walked in the store with a huge smile on his face. Leena watched every step he took as he approached them. Her stare drifted to his casual black slacks, hugging his strong hips.

"Good afternoon, Ladies." He turned to the older woman, "Lilly, how are you doing today? Leena, always still the observant one, I see." His smile told her he knew she checked his body out.

She blushed at being caught. "Hey Roger, what're you doing all the way down here?"

"Hello, Detective," giggled Lilly. "Look at what a secret admirer sent to our Leena. Isn't it beautiful?"

"Yes, I see. How fortunate for you, Sweetness. Remember, I told you yesterday I'd stop by and peek in on you, so it's what I'm doing. Is it okay with you?"

"Of course it is. You know I always enjoy seeing you. We were just discussing my gift. I can't believe someone saw me studying it and bought it for me. I'd love to go back and talk with the artist to ask about it. He left the shop in a hurry."

"I've got some free time this afternoon. Why don't we go together?" he suggested.

"Sounds great. I can probably leave in a couple of hours and have Tabby close for me."

"No problem," the girl yelled from across the room. "You can leave whenever you want. I've got things under control. If someone wants a reading, I'll schedule an appointment in the morning for you."

"Great, thanks, Tabby. Lilly, you want to come with us? It'd be fun," suggested Leena. She thought Lilly appeared uncomfortable when she declined her offer.

"I'm sorry, Babies, but I've several appointments starting in thirty minutes. I can't reschedule them. But you two have fun and make an exciting afternoon of it. Enjoy." The woman winked at her, nodded her head at Roger, and left.

The old fox was planning it so I'd be alone with him. I'll have to get back at her later.

"Okay, well, it's just us, I guess. Come up with me while I change into less noticeable clothes."

"I must say, you do make a gorgeous fortune teller. You can tell mine anytime," he replied.

"We'll go up the inside stairs…I'm leaving, Tabby. See you tomorrow and thanks."

She led him out the back door into the small hall containing the stairs. "Let me make sure this door is locked, then we'll go up."

Stepping up in front of him, she led the way slowly up each step.

"Stop staring at my ass," she laughed, teasing.

"How do I do that? It's such a sexy ass, too."

"You're such a naughty flirt," she joked, taking a step but catching her foot on the hem of her long skirt. It pulled her off balance, but thick, strong arms surrounded her, pulling her close to his body before she had a chance to fall. She could feel his arousal against her stomach and knew her troubles had just begun.

Their eyes met and locked. His lips looked so soft and tempting. She wanted to suck them into her mouth and lavish them with her tongue.

Chapter Thirteen

Roger's breath came faster against her face and she watched him lick his lips.

"You don't make it easy for a girl, do you?"

"Not you, I don't. You're going to have to say it out loud, Sweetness." His smile was wicked as he appeared to wait for her to answer.

She lifted her fingers, touching his hair.

God, how I want him right here.

Her fingers drifted down, brushing his cheek, and stroking across his bottom lip. Not wanting to move but knowing she must, she gently pulled free from the safety of his warm embrace, and turned to continue to climb.

"Thank you for catching me. Let me go ahead and change and we'll be off." Her ears picked up the large sigh he let escape. She winced at the thought of disappointing him, but she couldn't let things develop right now. There was too much to do.

****

Once inside, he sat at the kitchen table, musing over what could've occurred, while she went to her bedroom. He realized he shouldn't have encouraged her, but he wanted her. If they could just catch a break on the murders, then maybe they'd put the killer away, and it would all be over. The focus would then be on their relationship. She might not be ready, but he wasn't walking away.

"Penny for your thoughts?" she asked, studying his face.

"Not really worth much, I'm afraid."

Taking the hint he didn't want to discuss his thoughts, she changed the subject. "Can I offer you anything to drink before we head out?"

"No, I'm good. I can get something once we get to Jackson Square."

"Can we walk? It's a perfect day outside. Besides, there aren't many parking spots down there."

"Good idea. We can always catch a taxi back."

"Why, Mr. Black, are you saying you'll poop out on me?"

"Not at all, Miss Price, not at all. Ready?" He gave her a huge wink, holding the door open for her.

They made their way from Conti Street to Royal, taking it all the way to St. Peter's Street. He asked her several times if there were any stores they passed which she wanted to go into and look around. Surprised she kept turning him down, his curiosity finally got the best of him as they turned onto St. Peter's Street.

"I have to ask, Sweetness, are you at all normal? My experience has been most all women love to shop and

212

rarely turn down an opportunity. You've turned me down at least seven times since we started this journey."

She moved straight into his path and frowned into his face.

Uh oh, I've fucked up. Way to go, Roger, he thought. He could feel his face flush.

As he watched her, the corners of her luscious mouth lifted, finally breaking out in laughter.

"I had you worried, didn't I, Mr. Black? I don't think you could call me normal, but I do like to shop. I simply want to get to the Square and talk to the artist before he leaves for the day. You crack me up."

He grabbed her hand, holding it as they strolled down to Jackson Square. She led him over to St. Ann Street, once they reached the Square and moved down toward Decatur. They'd walked halfway down the street, when he felt her pull her hand out of his. She moved toward the fence where an artist had a large collection of paintings on the fence, as well as, stacked standing in several groups. What Roger determined were his better paintings were the ones attached to the fence and on a few easels.

"Hi, I hate to bother you, remember me?"

"Yes, I do. How could I forget someone as beautiful as you? I hope you enjoyed the sea captain."

"Exactly what I wanted to talk to you about. Oh, I'm sorry, this is my good friend, Roger Black." Roger nodded in his direction. "I was wondering if you could share any information about the person who bought the painting."

Roger was studying the artist, after shaking hands, and while he and Leena were talking. He was a young man, probably in his late twenties or early thirties. His hair was long and pulled back in a ponytail. He wore blue jeans, with a faded work shirt left open over a black wife beater T-shirt. Naturally, sandals were on his feet.

"I'm afraid I can't, Miss Leena. He paid me a lot of money beyond the cost of the painting in order to keep the transaction private. I'm really sorry."

"I understand. I was hoping you could share but I wouldn't want you to fault on the sale's restrictions. Can you tell me if he shared with you why he purchased it for me?"

"He simply stated you'd caught his eye admiring my art. He saw your face when you saw the sea captain and how disappointed you were when you walked away empty handed. He could tell you really wanted it. When we couldn't negotiate a price within your budget, he said he felt he had to purchase it for you. I do hope you're going to keep it and not return it?"

"Oh, I am. I couldn't part with it if I had to. Thank you so much for talking with me and telling me what you could."

"You're welcome, Miss. Enjoy the rest of your afternoon. It was nice to meet you, Roger."

Roger gave him a smile and a nod, grabbing her hand again.

"Since we're almost there, let's head over to Café Du Monde. Have you tried them yet?"

"Yes I have. I could use something to drink and I want a beignet. Let's go."

They crossed Decatur Street, stepped into the outdoor café, ordered, and then found a table at the far end of the café, overlooking the street and the Square. Placing the card with a number on it on its stand on the table, they talked about her painting, while waiting for their food.

Roger enjoyed watching her as she talked about things she loved. Her eyes twinkled, which lit up her entire face. He hadn't seen her this animated before and he loved it.

"So, you've no idea who's heart you bewitched enough to buy a painting for you?" unmercifully teasing her.

"I can count on one hand the number of people in New Orleans who know me." To prove her point, she counted her fingers, coming up with five people.

He delighted in teasing her, making her laugh out loud. She blushed again and it looked good on her.

At that moment, the waiter brought their beignets and drinks. They both settled into savoring the pastry, not realizing how hungry they were. They'd ordered four...two each. It didn't take long at all for the first one to disappear.

He detected she intently watched him cut into his pastry, placing a large bite on his fork. As he brought the bite to his mouth, he saw a mischievous grin spread across her face. Something was up, he thought, so he carefully observed her movements. She put the last beignet on her plate and nothing appeared out of the ordinary to him at all. He certainly hadn't done anything to warrant her scrutiny and evil smile. She picked the pastry up slowly with both hands, holding it level with her mouth, and before he could duck out of the way, she blew the powdered sugar all over his face. He'd scrunched his face up in enough time to protect his eyes and when he blew a sigh of relief from his mouth, sugar flew everywhere.

Leena was laughing so hard, tears were running down her cheeks.

"I wish you could see your face," she tried to tell him between her spasms of laughter.

"Oh, you think it's funny, do you?" picking up his beignet and blowing the powdered sugar across the table into her hair and face. She screamed and then they were both laughing loudly enough to become the interest of all eyes around them. They were the star attraction of customers at their end of the café. Neither one of them cared…it was too much fun.

Everyone's eyes moved from the couple, to the street as jazz played loudly moving toward them.

"Oh, this is a treat, Leena, you've got to see this. Come on." He pulled her up by her hands, helping brush off the sugar, and pulling her to the side of the street. Coming down St. Ann Street, then making a right turn at the corner, onto Decatur, were several musicians playing jazz music. They were followed by a bride and groom dressed to the nines, followed by a long string of people who were in the wedding party and guests. Dancing and marching, they rhythmically boogied their way to the building where the reception was going to be held.

"This is wonderful, Roger. It's so cool to see them enjoying themselves dancing in the street. Does this happen a lot?"

"Quite a bit. New Orleans loves to celebrate anything and any way they can. We do know how to throw a great party."

They watched the rest of the parade dance down the street, disappearing around the corner.

"I'm glad I got to see them. It looked fun. Oh look, there's a caricature artist over on the corner. Let's get him to draw us, please?"

"Let's see how good his work is first. I don't want to end up looking like a smurf." She pulled him by the arm, across the street. Running up to the artist, she asked how much he charged. Her excitement was so infectious, there was no way he could say no to her.

He had to admit, the guy was good. Roger sat in a chair and she sat on his lap with her arms around his neck. The artist finished the picture in about thirty to forty minutes. Roger paid him thirty dollars and the artist rolled it up, placing it in a cardboard tube to protect it. It was good enough, Roger intended to frame it and hang it in his bedroom.

He took her hand once more, pulling her toward a restaurant at the corner of St. Peter and Decatur. "Have you ever had a Jax Burger?"

"Um, no, I'm afraid I haven't."

"Well, then you're in for a super treat. Angus beef smothered in Jax's own homemade beer sauce and topped with onion straws. We're going to order two to go and have a picnic at Woldonberg Park. You'll never be the same."

It was four forty-five by the clock on the wall of the Jackson Brewery Bistro Bar. They drank a beer while waiting for their order to be prepared.

"We need to come back one day when we can sit down and eat here. They even have a dance floor."

"It's really pretty in here. I like the ambience of the place. Very nice but not stuffy."

"Well, you're going to get some down to earth ambience this evening." He winked at her as they brought out a large paper bag containing their order. Once he paid for the food, he turned to her still sitting on the chair.

"Come with me. We're going to sit by the mighty Mississippi River and eat our burgers."

They walked down the sidewalk until they found an empty bench. He proceeded to unpack the bag, pulling out tons of French fries along with the huge burgers. It was a feast. They'd also put in two bottles of water for them.

"There's no way I can eat all of this. It's enough for an army."

"Simply sit here, eat, drink, and be merry. We'll watch the river all laid back and satisfied."

"You paint a very tempting picture. Did you purchase the painting?"

"No, as much as I'd love to take credit, I probably couldn't afford it. You'll have to come up with someone else."

"Oh well, back to the drawing board"

.

Chapter Fourteen

The two sat quietly, ate their food, and watched barges going up and down the Mississippi. Leena fell back against the back of the bench, heaved a contented sigh, and wiped her mouth with a napkin.

"You're right. The burger was delicious but I can't possibly finish it. I'm stuffed."

"Put it back in the box and we'll carry the leftovers back to the apartment in the bag.

Watching the tour boat pass by them heading down the river, she leaned back and smiled at him.

"I'd have thought you were an implant to NOLA."

"Why is that?" She had his full attention now.

"The way you always eat beef when we've eaten together. I've never seen you pick seafood once."

"Ah, well, I do like seafood but I love good beef more. What about you? You like sea food?"

"Not so much. I like fried shrimp but that's about it. I love Italian food and different pastas."

"I'll have to remember for future reference."

"So tell me, how long have you lived in New Orleans?"

"All my life. I was born and raised here."

"So you've family still here?"

"Yep, my pops passed away three years ago, but my mom, three sisters, and their families are all here."

Her face lit up with a teasing smile. "You were the only boy? How was that for you?"

Roger perked his head up, laughing out loud. "Yes, I was and the youngest too. They loved their baby brother."

"What made you choose homicide for a profession or did you simply want to kill your sisters?" She laughed with him and could tell he knew it wasn't at him.

"My dad was an undercover detective. He worked the drug end of the business but it definitely overlapped. It's where I was introduced to homicide. I guess I just fell in love with the hunt and investigation. Went to college to gain background knowledge, then studied, took, and passed the detective exam. I was partnered with Bryan and I've been with him since. We work well together…he's bad ass and I'm the diplomat."

"No kidding. He's definitely the bad cop of your duo."

"Yeah, he's gruff and questions everything, but it's what makes him so good. He doesn't miss much. What about you? How did you get interested in Tarot or is there something you'd rather do?"

"Well, let's see, my mother was my protector and cheerleader. She died when I was six. My father was the pastor of a Holy Roller church and his favorite sermon was the wide road to Hell. He always told me how evil I was because of my gift. Thankfully, my mom had instilled her belief in God and how much He loved His children."

Warmth spread through her when Roger took her hand into his. She smiled into his eyes and continued.

"I left home at fifteen, lived on the street. It was difficult trying to survive and hide at the same time. There wasn't any proof my father looked for me, which tells me a great deal."

"Is he still alive?"

"As far as I know, he is. I don't particularly care. Anyway, after a year, I went to stay with my mom's family for a while. I think you already know they were gypsies. After eight months, I left them and went back to the street, a little tougher and wiser. I took different jobs to pay my own way and moved on when I needed to."

"What was wrong with living with your mom's family?"

"They like their women married and in the home. A twenty-six year old male had his heart set on taking me for a wife. He worked hard to gain the council's agreement. Since I have a problem with male dominance, I left before it was forced on me. I was close to eighteen, so they couldn't stop me."

"You know, a lot of girls aren't as lucky?"

"I know, but they weren't as entrenched in the old ways as some were. I was fortunate. After a few of years doing odd jobs and staying in cheap hotels, I wanted a more stable life. I longed to have someone around me who truly loved me with all my faults. So, I came to New Orleans to be with my Nana."

She looked back at the river, noticing it had become dark. Dropping his hand, she rose from the bench and stood.

"We'd better head back home. It's dark and I've got to get up early."

Roger pushed up from his seat and picked up the bag. "Do you want to walk or should I call a taxi?"

"Let's take a taxi, if you don't care. I'm still rather full."

They hiked back to Jackson's, called, and waited out front for the taxi.

Roger leaned his body against the building with one foot perched back against the bricks. An old familiar tingle sped like lightening through her. He looked hot, standing there all manly, and she wanted to jump him. Leena knew if she let him walk her to her door, she wouldn't let him go home. Tonight, she couldn't let it happen. She needed an excuse and before they got there.

The taxi arrived and they scrambled into the back. Roger made small talk with the driver, while she racked her brain for a reason to not let him go in with her. It didn't take long to pull in front of the shop, and after paying the fare, they stood in front of the store, staring into each other's eyes. She cleared her throat, preparing to start her impromptu speech, when he interrupted her.

"Leena, this is as far as I go tonight. I'll wait until you get inside and turn your lights on. If I walk you in, I won't go home."

He pulled her against his chest, wrapping his arms tightly around her, and breathed heavily into her hair. "The surveillance car is down the street so I feel pretty safe in saying the apartment and store are secure. I'll say my goodbye…right here," moving his lips within an inch of hers. "Right now."

His mouth consumed hers, forcing his tongue inside, sucking at her very soul. Her tingles exploded into throbs, beating her very life throughout her body. She held tightly to his hair, threading her fingers through it, pulling him closer and sucking his tongue into her mouth.

They broke apart, panting and laughing at the whistles and cat calls they received.

"I think you better go up before we create a scene."

"I think we already did. I had fun with you tonight, Roger. Thank you."

"My pleasure, Ma'am. Always willing to brighten your day." He kissed her quickly once more, then let her go. She knew when she reached the landing of the stairs, he would still be standing at the bottom, watching her. Sure enough, there he stood, waiting for her to turn the key and walk in.

Once inside, she secured the door, moved straight to her bedroom, and out onto the balcony. He'd moved to the front of the shop and smiled up at her.

"Good night, Sweetness, Sleep well."

"Good night, Roger...you too." He walked to his car, half a block away, and drove off.

I'm so screwed. He's gone and stole my heart.

****

Leena awoke, feeling really great. Nightmares hadn't plagued her, so she'd slept deeply all night. Her skirt from the day before, lay draped across the chair. She chose a black peasant blouse this time and kept everything else the same.

Her footsteps were light and springy this morning as she flew down the stairs. Tabby was already blessing the shop, which gave her great comfort.

I like this girl...we can teach each other a lot.

She unlocked the register, taking yesterday's cash, checks, and receipts, and placed them in the bank bag. Tabby had already checked off and totaled everything, so they'd be ready this morning for the bank courier to pick up first thing.

The girl finished her ritual and went over to the counter.

"You've got an appointment for a reading this morning at ten o'clock."

"Good. Male or female, young or old?"

"Female and young," responded Tabby.

"Okay, unlock the door and let's start this day."

From nine until ten, the shop wasn't busy, giving Leena time to prepare herself and her room. Tabby sat behind the counter, reading a magazine while she waited for a customer.

When Leena finished energizing her room, she went and sat on a bar stool, next to the young witch. She really liked the girl and wanted to know more about her.

"How long have you lived in New Orleans, Tabby?"

"About ten years now, I guess. I moved here with my parents. Once I graduated, I moved in with my boyfriend against my parents' wishes."

"You still live with him?"

"Yeah, I do. My parents thought it'd never last, but we're still hot for each other. We've been together six years. They finally started talking to him two years ago."

"I'm glad it worked out for you. I know how some parents can be."

Just then, the bell over the door rang, and a young blonde wearing a ponytail, tottered into the shop.

"This is your appointment," Tabby whispered to her.

Leena put a huge smile across her face and spoke. "Welcome, may we help you?"

"I've a ten o'clock appointment to have my fortune read with Madame Leena."

She chuckled to herself. "You're right on time and it's just Leena. There's no Madame here. Come on back and let's see what we can find out for you."

Her cell phone buzzed and saw it was Roger. "Go ahead and go on in. Take the seat on the left side of the table. This will only take me a minute."

"Hi Roger. How was your night?"

"One of the best I've had in a while. I owe it to you," he replied.

"Me too…no nightmares."

"I've only got a second. I want to go to the club tonight and see if anyone's heard anything. Will you come with me? Do you still have the clothes Lilly gave you?"

"Yes and yes."

"Good. I'll pick you up at seven thirty. Bye Sweetness."

She clicked her phone completely off, and went up the steps into her reading room. Sitting across from the girl, she reached for her cards, shuffling them in her hands while she talked. "So what are you wanting to find out today? What are you looking for?"

"I just had my first date with this guy. I met him a month ago and I really like him. I want to know if we'll fall in love with each other."

"I'm assuming this would be a good thing?" she asked the young blonde.

"Oh, yes, it would be perfect."

"What I want you to do is take this deck of cards, hold them in your hands for a moment, and then shuffle them. Think about what you just told me and when you feel as if the deck is thoroughly shuffled, hand them back to me."

She observed the girl take great care with the cards, while completely mixing them over and over. Finally, she smiled at Leena and handed them to her.

Taking the deck, the fortune teller placed one card face up on the table. The next card, she placed face up to the left of the first, and then the last, face up to the left of the second. Then she placed a fourth card face down above all three cards.

"I'm doing a three card spread unless we need to go further and that's what the upside down card is for. Usually, it's not needed but you never know. The first card is the Magician…a very powerful card. You see how he's staring straight at us, almost as if he is concentrating on us? In his hands, he controls the four elements of the Tarot…cups, wands, swords, and pentacles. Basically, you've everything you need to accomplish what you want. The light over his head links together the earth and heavens. It is a very good and powerful card."

"This is so exciting. What's the next one?" the blonde asked.

"The High Priestess is next. Again, an extremely powerful card. While the Magician was male, the Priestess is female. They are equal in power and are one of the two most potent couples in the deck. She's draped in a transparent veil and appears to be in a trance, floating above the water. She wears a mask with stars adorning her hair. You see the crescent moon behind her head? It, along with the stars, enables her to reach a higher plane for knowledge. The mask represents mystery and secrets. She's showing you, you've the ability to find a deeper answer to the mystery within you. Coupled with the Magician, you've tremendous power to obtain what you seek."

The girl giggled like a child at Christmas, bobbing up and down in her chair. Her enthusiasm made Leena laugh inside, fighting hard not to let it explode outward.

"Now, this last card is the Two of Cups. You can see we've a male and female staring intently into each other's eyes. A light is above their heads, circling down into each of the cups. This is the card of union. It suggests the growth of a relationship into a blissful and harmonious bond."

She looked up and the young girl was smiling with tears running down her cheeks. Leena smile back.

"I think the prospect of falling in love is excellent. We won't need the fourth card. Do you have any questions you want to ask me?"

"No, I think you've answered everything for me. Thank you so much. What do I owe you?"

"Whatever you feel like giving. There is no set charge. Just pay Tabby up front what you think it was worth. Holler at me if she's busy helping customers. I'm glad you're happy with the outcome. Have a blessed day."

The rest of the morning was uneventful until an older, distraught woman came in wanting a reading. The woman was crying loudly so Leena rose from her stool and helped her into her Tarot room. The woman explained she'd been worried her marriage of fifteen years, was over. She asked Leena if she would be able to find the answer.

Her gut told her it wouldn't be a pleasant reading, but she couldn't refuse the poor woman. Sure enough, the three cards pulled were the Devil card, the Four of Wands, and the Death card. The lady totally freaked when Leena turned over the Death card and placed it face up on the table. She reassured the woman it wasn't what she thought. However, she knew in her heart it wasn't a stress free reading.

Great detail was given to the woman about each card, explaining the mood, forces, and direction. She'd always been one to give truth to her customers or friends she read for, so she wouldn't sugar coat this one. She explained to her the situation with her marriage was dragging her down and keeping her in emotional bondage. Through her own choice, the woman was forcing herself to remain in a loveless marriage which would go nowhere. However, through the Four of Wands card, she could celebrate knowing new things…good things, were on the horizon. The Death card symbolizes change in her life. Even if fear of change claimed her, she could believe when one phase of our life ends, it makes way for a new one. It was the opportunity available to the woman.

She spent an hour and a half with the depressed lady, but by the time she gave all of her interpretations, the woman left the shop satisfied. The whole ordeal exhausted Leena

.

Chapter Fifteen

The shelves needed to be restocked and she jumped in to help Tabby. The girl gave her helpful hints on how to remember what items went together and which ones didn't.

When four o'clock arrived, Leena left the shop, went upstairs to shower, and unwind before Roger picked her up. She didn't know what made her say yes about the club, other than the fact she wanted to see him. Maybe it would be a quick meet and greet, letting her quickly go in and out.

Yeah, right, I've a strong feeling he has plans for me and I don't think I'll like it, she thought.

The outfit Lilly loaned her had been folded and placed in her bureau. She'd 'bodscaped' herself in the shower, so she reluctantly pulled open the drawer. There it was, simply laying on top, mocking her. Or so she imagined.

Yeah, you got me this time, but I'm making a vow this will be the last time I wear you in public.

The bustier still fit like a glove along with the panties. She stood in front of the mirror and gave herself a big smile. Her reflection was hot.

"Hot or not, I still won't do this again," she told herself.

Even though it wasn't cool outside, she grabbed her coat from the closet, marched into the living room, and plopped in front of the television to wait for Roger.

Some crazy reality show was on cable, when her phone buzzed, indicating she'd received a text. 'Going on break for an hour for dinner. Put the *Back in an Hour* sign on the door and locked it. Will close shop at eight…Tabby.

The time on her phone was six o'clock, so she thought she could stretch out and get comfortable. With her head propped up on a pillow, she scooted her hips around, and pulled her feet onto the couch. The background noise of the television lulled her into a dreamlike state.

Her mind was drifting from reality to fantasy. Roger was there, all decked out in leather, and staring at her intently enough to make her cream her panties. When he stared that way, he controlled her…body, thoughts, and physical reactions.

A wicked smile crossed his face, then suddenly, he faded away. Saddened because he left, she'd been standing and discovered her body was immobile. Arms felt crossed over her chest and wrapped tightly to it. Knees were shoved up into her face and felt held in place by an unknown force. However, when she looked down at herself, she stood in the same position as when she started.

Panic filled her dream before she jerked awake when a loud commercial woke her up. Sweat drops on her face, neck, and upper body, cooled her off to the point of being chilled.

Afternoon naps don't help me at all.

Standing up, she slipped into her coat, wrapping it around her, and trying to warm her body. Someone knocked on the door. The clock over the television showed seven twenty-five so she knew it had to be Roger.

His eyes took her body in, when she opened the door. His face appeared puzzled to her, as if he wondered what the hell she had on.

"Leena, honey, what's with the coat? It's the middle of summer."

"I know it is. I had the coat out to wear tonight so my body would be covered when we go to the club. I laid down, fell asleep, and had a bad dream. Sweat covered me and when I woke up, I started freezing. Hence, I put the coat on for warmth."

"Okay, makes sense. Are you ready to go?"

"Yeah, I think so. What's the plan tonight?"

They stepped out the door together and he waited for her to lock up. He always opened the car door for her and it thrilled her. She loved how he always took care of her.

"Um, plans?"

"Oh, yeah. Tonight I'm simply taking you through the dungeon on the premise we're looking for your interests to try. We'll walk through the scenes, pretend to discuss them, and I'll talk with different workers and see if any gossip about the murders has gone around."

"So, no plans to put me on the spot and embarrass me into doing a scene?"

"No way. What kind of Dom do you take me for? I'd never do that to you. Consensual…remember? You know me better than that, Leena."

"I do…I'm sorry, Roger. Just nervous, I guess. You were in my dream and you held me immobile, literally frozen in place by your Dom persona. It made me uncomfortable."

"I can understand why, but you know I'm not that way."

"Yes."

He parked the car in front of the Secret Whispers Club and turned to her. "Sit still. I want to open your door before you go ahead and hop out."

"Okay?" she answered, questioning his motive.

When he opened her door, she swung her legs out, pulling the coat partially open. He held his hand out to her and helped her stand.

"I wanted to watch your beautiful body slide out of my car." He wrapped his arms around her waist, pulling her against him. "Now let's go search for information," his lips pressed hard against her, as his tongue danced with hers.

"Whoa, keep doing what you're doing and I won't be able to stand."

"That was my plan. After you, Sweetness."

They checked in at the front desk and once again, Paul was on duty.

"Well, hello beautiful. Are you here with Roger or simply as a guest? Please tell me it's as a guest so I know there's a chance we'll play later." His face was all smiles as he spoke to her.

Her eyes went wide as she turned to Roger for help.

"Afraid she's with me, Paul. We're here basically to see what appeals to our beautiful girl."

Paul smiled, put his hands in the air, admitting defeat.

"You all enjoy yourselves."

Roger placed his hands on her shoulders, helped her remove her coat, and hung it up. From behind them, he could hear a distinct 'mmmhmmm'.

"I think you're being appreciated."

"I think you need to stay close to me."

"I agree. Now, become a sub and behave yourself."

"Yes, Sir."

Rather than take the elevator, he escorted her down the stairs to the dungeon. The first couple they came to were involved in a flogging scene. The woman was bent over a spanking bench with her wrists cuffed to the opposing side. Her ass was arched into the air, letting her Dom have easy access to her sex and all necessary parts.

Leena couldn't imagine being in her position in front of others. She really did have a difficult time with public nudity.

Roger struck up conversations with two of his fellow on-site Doms. She, on the other hand, was mesmerized by the way the Dom was using the flogger to arouse his sub. He struck her ass cheek, then slowly and gently, drug the strands of the flogger over her pussy. By the way the sub squirmed, Leena could see she enjoyed what he did. Over and over, he would flog her ass, then stroke her pussy.

Unable to help herself, Leena was aroused as well. Watching the scene was hot and once the sub moaned, Leena squirmed standing next to Roger. She tried to be inconspicuous, but she noted he stared at her, smirking.

"Leena, see something you might like?"

Lowering her head, she politely answered, "Yes, Sir."

"Very good. Come on, let's keep walking. I'll give you a report later tonight when we leave."

He stopped in front of an alcove where a couple was using the St. Andrews Cross. The sub was naked and attached to the cross with her back to her Dom. He cracked a bullwhip, making his sub and everyone else near, jump.

Leena lowered her head and refused to look. It reminded her too much of the night she watched another couple whose sub ended up being the second victim.

Another Dom strolled up to the same alcove, and started chatting with Roger.

"Master James, it's good to see you. How've you been?"

"Very busy. You know how much I like to teach young men to be a Dom. We're increasing in numbers weekly. Says something about our club and curriculum."

"Says a lot about our teacher, Sir."

"You're very kind, Roger. All of my Doms here are talented. I see you've a new protégé. Miss Leena, it's good to see you again. How've you been?"

"Thank you, Sir. I'm doing well."

"Little One, you may raise your eyes here." She looked up into his face and smiled. "Very good, Leena."

While he and Roger talked about the club, she studied Master James. He was tall and well built. It was hard to tell how muscled his body was, since he wore a suit, but if his hips were any indication, he was ripped. His hair was dark brown with wisps of silver at the sides. Eyes were a deep brown and warmth seemed to radiate from them.

Simply looking at him, you'd never know he ran the dungeon with an iron grip...very friendly and outgoing.

He caught her staring at him and she blushed from embarrassment. She immediately ducked her head.

"No, no, no, Little One," placing a leather gloved hand under her chin, lifting her face. "You're welcome to study my face. If you get tired of my friend, here, let me know and I'll be delighted to play with you."

"I doubt it'll happen, Old Friend," Roger reacted.

"Say, Roger, do you and Leena have plans for Saturday night? I'd like to have you both over for dinner and cook for you. I won't take no for an answer, unless of course, you do have plans."

"What do you think, Leena? Think we should give this old man an opportunity to cook for us?"

"Yes, Sir, I think we probably should. Thank you, Master James."

"You're very welcome, Sweet Girl. Rog, I'll see the two of you at seven Saturday night. And Leena, we won't stand on Dom/s protocol. Simply be yourself."

He strolled away with a flare no one else in the club possessed. His persona automatically commanded respect from everyone he came in contact with. Yet, he still was warm and pleasant…a real person.

They spent another hour wandering around, talking with different people. Finally, Roger suggested they leave. As they approached the car, he turned and faced her.

"What do you say we stop and get a pizza?"

"Like this? No way."

"I mean order one to go, Goof Ball. This outfit is for my eyes only, thank you very much."

"Yours and the people at the club, don't forget."

"That'll change, from now on. I'll go through the drive through. You got drinks at home?"

"Beer and colas."

"Good enough." He proceeded to a nearby pizza parlor, placed his order at the drive-through, and pulled up in line to wait on their order.

"Did anyone tell you anything they'd heard about the murders?"

"Not many. James said he'd heard talk among the local club owners, it was someone definitely into BDSM, but was possibly linked with the vampire and occult communities as well."

"Well, seems to cover a huge portion of New Orleans. Not much to go on."

"We'll keep trying, Sweetness." He brushed his hand across her cheek. "Don't lose hope. The perp's bound to mess up sooner or later."

"It needs to be sooner, Roger, before we lose another one to this guy."

"I know, Baby…I know."

When they pulled up to the window, their pizza was ready. He paid for it and took off toward the apartment.

****

Up in her apartment, Roger watched her set two places at the table with plates, napkins, and beer.

"Do you mind if I change clothes into something less revealing?"

His mind drifted back to the great sex they'd had and he had to smile.

"Go ahead, but hurry. You don't want cold pizza."

"I will, but I do have a microwave. Be back in a second."

His eyes followed her as she sauntered into her bedroom and closed the door. His pulse quickened and his crotch tightened. He wanted her, but figured he'd better behave himself. After all, she made herself very clear the last time, she didn't want a relationship.

He sighed, looking up as her door opened, and lost it all when she strolled back into the kitchen. She'd changed into a man's large white dress shirt long enough to barely cover her ass.

God, those incredible legs. I want to crawl my way up those beautiful thighs.

"Go ahead and eat, don't wait on me," Leena coaxed.

Chapter Sixteen

Leena had no idea what had gotten into her, but from the look on Roger's face, he liked it. Butterflies were swimming in her gut, but from the moment he watched her exit his car, she realized she wouldn't let him go home tonight. Not if she had anything to do with it.

His eyes were playful and she gave him a huge smile as she put a piece of pizza on her plate. It was cold, so she took it, popped it in the microwave, and stood with her back to him.

Warmth floated over the back of her body. She sensed him standing close to her and jumped when his hands brushed their way up her thighs. Lips pressed into her hair, near her ear, and his breath was hot on her skin.

"Did you wear this for me, baby?" His lips kissed down her neck and across to the nape, where he licked, then blew his breath across it. A moan, deep from her throat, escaped her lips. She fell against him, melting.

"I'll take that as a yes. You're so sexy, Sweetness. Don't make me go home tonight."

The microwave notified her the pizza was ready. She took it off the plate, and slowly turned her body to face him. He pressed her up against the counter, pinning her with his arms.

"Bite?" she asked, offering him the pizza.

His eyes locked onto hers as he opened his mouth and bit off the end.

"I'm not letting you leave tonight, Sir. You've started a fire in me and I need it put out." Her hips rubbed against his, and in turn, his eyes glazed over and his breath hitched.

Leena moaned once more, rolling her head back. Taking advantage of the opening, he trailed his mouth up her throat, to her chin, and finding her lips, devoured them. In one quick movement, he grabbed her ass, set her on the cabinet, and pulled her close to the edge.

"No panties? Oh, woman, you make me burn. I'd love to extinguish your fire and start it all over again. God help me, I want to be inside you right now."

Her fingers fumbled with the zipper of his leather pants, but finally pulled them down. She grabbed both sides of his pants, pulled and tugged, until they were down to his knees. His cock stood proud, curving up between them.

He unbuttoned her shirt and helped her remove it. His fingers were tender, cupping and stroking her breasts. She loved how he seemed to worship them with his hands. When his mouth surrounded her nipple and began sucking, she lost all concentration on exploring his cock. Her back arched against his face, fingers gripped his hair, and pulled his head closer.

His fingers trailed down the slope and curve of her body to her pussy, stroking between her lips, and bathing in her honey. He grabbed her ass with force, and pulled her off the cabinet, slamming her against his cock. Her arms immediately wound around his neck for support, but she eventually managed to work her hand down between them, and position his dick at her entrance. With a mighty groan, he thrust up inside her.

"Unngh," the force of his thrust caused great pleasure to flow through her sex. She held off the orgasm about to flood over her.

"Again," she moaned.

"Yes," he replied, thrusting again as her arms held on tight.

"Look at me, baby. Leena, open your eyes. We're going to cum together, eye to eye." He thrust twice more and she fought to keep her eyes open.

"Don't hold back, Roger. I'm so close, let me have it all."

He maneuvered her back against the wall, then let his body take control. He slammed into her over and over.

Once Roger let himself go, her body took over, building and climbing. His cock rubbed against her clit and hit her sweet spot at the same time. The pleasure was intense and was all she could focus on. It took over, working for release, until her body went rigid and exploded all over him.

His pounding accelerated, legs were trembling, then stopped, and she sensed the warmth of his cum filling her and dripping down.

He didn't know if he could do it, but he attempted to carry her into her bedroom. Even though his knees were strained and weak, he managed to make it in there and lay her on the bed.

When he laid next to her, she curled and wrapped herself around him. They both were out of breath and tired, but the coming down from the mountain part, was perfect snuggling against him. What changed her heart, she wondered.

It didn't matter. This was where she wanted to be, so if she'd opened herself up for hurt, so be it.

"You're deep in thought, Sweetness. I hope they're all for me." He stroked his hands up and down her hip and thigh. The slow rhythm he used, lulled her to the brink of sleep. All she could think of was how he knew the right ways to make her feel good.

"Climb up here and let me feel your body cover mine." When she obeyed, he groaned, stroked her ass, and smile up at her. "Mmm, you feel wonderful. I'm ready to go again, but I'm taking my time only for you. Every inch of your body will enjoy the talents of my tongue and mouth. Here, get on your hands and knees, scoot up and straddle my face."

Her face blushed as she crawled up his body. She planted her sex over his face, and he held on to her ass, squeezing and massaging the cheeks. His breath on her pussy was warm and occasionally, he would lick her slit.

"That's good, baby. Now place your hands on the headboard for support. I'm going to eat you as if I were starved, because for you, I am. You have permission to grind against my face and ride my tongue anyway that gets you off. If it feels good, then do it."

She lost control of her hips when he ran his tongue over her lips, pointing and circling around her clit. They undulated in small circles, trying to match the circular motion of his magnificent oral tool. He thrust it into her canal, drinking the honey flowing into his face. The moist touch of his fleshy muscular organ, thrusting in and out, pleasured and stimulated her. Then, her body took control, pumping against his face.

Her hands gripped the headboard, as she lifted and lowered her pussy to his mouth. Sensual sounds of licks, kisses, smacking, and sucking drove her further to the edge, until she soared off the cliff. She screamed as her orgasm pulsed through her body.

"Oh, my God, Roger, don't stop. Please."

He didn't. He grabbed her hips, forcing her sex against his mouth, relentlessly flicking her nub, until she crested again.

"I'm cumming again…yes, oh God, yes."

She heard the faint sound of chuckling, as he continued to suck and nibble. At the same time, he placed his finger on her puckered hole, slowly circling it.

"Oh please," she moaned, building again while he continued his assault of erotic bliss. He slid his finger through her juices, then went back to circling her rosette. Sucking once more on her nub, her hips danced to his pace, building a fire in her pussy. When she approached the peak, he placed his finger on her hole and gently pushed it in.

"Roger…oh, baby…that's so good." His hands held her in place, while her body drifted down into sweet oblivion. Then, he flipped her over on her back, placed his cock at her entrance, and slammed into her, thrusting until his own orgasm exploded over him. His grunts and groans told her he'd had his own blissful ride.

He collapsed on top of her and she rubbed his back, secretly enjoying touching him. They were covered in sweat.

"I don't want to, Sweetness, but I've got to roll off and cool down."

"Thank you," she answered. "I didn't think you'd ever roll over. I'm burning up." They broke out in laughter, laying side by side, and eventually fell asleep.

****

Sometime during the night, Roger woke up and scooted over near her. Pushing up on his elbow, he studied her face while she slept. How I got lucky enough to warrant her attention, I'll never know, he thought. The moonlight drifted across her body through spaces in the curtains. Her beauty melted him. He lay beside her, in awe of her street smarts, but it was her innocence which captured him. She wasn't ready to hear him tell her he loved her, but he also knew, he'd captured her heart.

Her skin was soft, tanned, and he craved it. He brushed his finger tip down her cheek and across her lips. Awestruck, he couldn't stop touching her. Her eyes slowly opened and blinked. He gazed into beautiful emerald eyes, which took his breath away.

"My beautiful woman, how on earth does that happen?"

"How does what happen?" she asked.

"Your eyes are a gorgeous shade of green. How do you do it?"

"I don't do it, Roger. They change on their own. Usually, it's when I have a vision, but I've got a feeling you changed them tonight. The sex was sensual, naughty, and so hot. I think they changed because you made me feel wonderful. It's just a guess, but I think a good one."

"What do you say to making them go a shade greener?"

"I'd say, you're on. I could have sex with you all night."

He pulled her into his arms, once more coaxing her body to respond to his skills. They made love twice more before falling into a heavy, deep sleep.

When the sun rose and peeked through the curtains, Roger slid off the bed moving into the bathroom. He then rummaged through the refrigerator gathering eggs, milk, cheese, and butter. The breakfast menu would consist of a cheese omelet with buttered toast and juice. He intended to serve her breakfast in bed and wake her with the surprise.

He dug through the cabinets for a frying pan, mixing bowl, found them, as well as an apron. Since he didn't take the time to put his pants back on, he considered he better at least wear an apron to cover his jewels. The bowl was large enough to make a six egg omelet. He busied himself with mixing the batter and heating the butter in the frying pan.

There was a toaster on the opposite cabinet, so he popped two pieces of bread into it. Then, he poured the batter into the pan, letting it solidify before adding the cheese. Once the egg mixture appeared to be congealed, he sprinkled the cheese on. The cheese melted and he flipped one side of the omelet on top of the other, letting it brown more.

He used the bottom of a broiler pan as a make-shift tray, placing two plates each containing one half omelet, one slice buttered toast, and two glasses of orange juice. Still asleep when he walked into the room, he placed the food on the top of her bureau, and sat by her on the bed.

For some odd reason, he thought of Sleeping Beauty, and gave the sleeping princess a kiss on the lips. She stirred, opened her eyes, and smiled up at him.

"Good morning, Roger. Did you get any sleep?"

"Good morning, Sweetness. Yes, I did. The sun woke me up and I decided to bring you a surprise."

He rose off the bed, collected the tray, and set it on the chair, moving the chair near the side of the bed. "Breakfast in bed, M'Lady."

"Roger, how sweet of you. This looks delicious and I'm famished. Someone kept me up all night and I worked up a big appetite."

They ate their breakfast quietly, enjoying each other's company. While Leena finished hers, Roger rose from the side of the bed, picking up his pants. Before he made his way to the bathroom, she stopped eating.

"Roger, are you wearing an apron?" and she began laughing. "I've never been served a meal by someone whose ass cheeks are hanging out and dangling bits exposed. You're awfully cute."

He smiled at her humor, went into the bathroom, shutting the door. He slipped on his pants, ran some water through his hair, and rinsed his mouth. When he strolled back into the room, she'd gotten up from the bed and stood stretching naked in front of the window. He stepped up to her, caressing her cheek.

"You keep this up and we'll be back in bed." He kissed her on the cheek, then looked for his shirt, throwing it on.

"I need to go home before I go into work. I'll try to stop by this evening but I can't promise you I will. We've got a meeting tonight to go over details about the serial killer. We're making sure we haven't missed anything. Either way, I'll call you. I'll probably call you several times today simply to hear your voice. Take care, Love, and come lock the door after I leave."

He kissed her and then waited for her to follow him.

She threw the locks and then jumped back into bed, only to

remember she had to work.

Chapter Seventeen

Leena sprinted through her morning routine and flew down the stairs. She had a few more appointments on her schedule. Word of mouth works wonders with local people. So she guessed both women discussed her with their friends. She even had one of her aunt's former clients come in and give her a try. The reading went well, thankfully, and the man appeared to leave satisfied.

They were busy in the morning with her three readings, but slowed down around lunch time. She sat behind the counter with Tabby, and talked.

"You know, the way you walked in here this morning, Boss Lady, I'd swear you got some last night."

Leena blushed bright red. "Boss Lady? Where did that come from?" feigning shock.

Tabby pressed on. "Uh, huh, I knew it. You did. Way to go, Girl Friend. It's about fucking time."

She sat and stared at the young girl, then threw her head back, roaring with laughter.

"Come on, I want details."

"Yes, I did the nasty last night…several times. How could you tell?"

"Your face. It glowed and the way you carried yourself, when you came in. For weeks, it's been as if you carried a heavy load in your arms. You're always polite, but never stepped outside of yourself. This morning, the load is gone and you're walking on air. You look beautiful."

"Aw, thank you, Tabby. And you know what? We're girlfriends, so no more Boss Lady or Miss Leena. It's simply Leena. Okay?"

"Okay." Tabby reached around her, giving her a hug.

Leena's cell phone buzzed. She looked at the screen and it was Roger, checking up on her. "How's it going today?" She blushed again and answered. "Me, too."

Tabby snuck to the other side of the store, to give her privacy to talk. Business picked up, so the lunch time lull was over.

Leena had two more appointments and spent the rest of the afternoon working the cash register. Later in the day, she helped the young witch restock and found herself remembering quite a few things she'd been taught. She was proud of herself.

"Hey Tabby, it's five thirty. You've covered for me many times closing up shop, why don't you take off early and go have a special night with your roomie?"

"Seriously? You'll be okay alone?"

"I'll be fine. You go and lighten your own load."

"Thanks, I'm going to take you up on your offer."

"Enjoy," she shouted, watching her leave.

Luckily, the crowds were thinning outside, so she sat behind the counter. A few stragglers came in, bought items, and left. But for the most part, business was pleasantly slow.

Thirty minutes before closing, she browsed through a magazine, and the doorbell rang. Bradly strolled in, approaching the counter.

"It looks as if things are going well for you. I thought you had a helper?"

"I do. I let her leave early for a change. She's earned it. How are you, Bradly?"

"Busy as always. I stopped by for two things. One, to see if you'd forgotten about our plans to go to dinner and two, to check if you started doing readings yet. You remember I told you I came to your aunt for advice quite often?"

"Yes, I remember, and yes, I have. I can't do it tonight, but when would you like to come in?"

"Why don't we try tomorrow, Friday? Say, at eleven in the morning?"

"Perfect," and she wrote it down in her appointment book. "I don't have any others around this time, so we can take our time."

"Now, what about dinner?"

Leena winced, but quickly recovered. "I'm not sure. Things are kind of crazy because of the murders. I want to find the killer. Basically, it's all I think about."

"I understand, there's no rush. I'm a patient man. Well, I'll let you close and see you in the morning at eleven."

"I'll be here," smiling as he left. "Oh crap, not good, not good."

Her phone buzzed with a voice mail from Roger. "Hey Sweetness, this meeting is going to run late, so I won't be able to come by. I'll see you tomorrow, I promise. I miss you. Bye."

Disappointed he couldn't come tonight, she at least was happy he'd called several times during the day. The time on the phone was ten minutes after eight. She stood, wandered to the door and flipped the neon sign outside, off. Then, she locked the door and pulled the blinds.

The adrenalin from last night finally wore off, and exhaustion controlled her. She'd eat a salad and then watch some television in bed. Fastest way for her to fall asleep. Hitting the light switch by the back door, she locked it and climbed the stairs.

The next morning, Leena awoke and wasn't as perky. Her body didn't feel like it had rested at all. She dragged through her morning routine and when she walked into the store, Tabby had a shocked look on her face.

"Are you okay? You look awful."

"I tossed and turned all night, but I didn't have any nightmares. I've got one appointment at eleven. Do you know if I have any others?

"I didn't make any."

"Good. If I make it through this day, it'll be a miracle."

"Well, then, we won't let it pull you down. We'll party all day. We can have several pizzas delivered...enough to share with customers. Plus, sweet tea and chocolate chip cookies. What do you think?" Tabby suggested.

"It sounds great. I'm all for having a party today. I can run up and make our own sweet tea. I'm sure I saw several gallon jars Nana cleaned out and stored. I've got a couple of hours before Bradly arrives, so I'll be back."

"I'll call a caterer, a friend I know, who's good and cheap, at least for me."

An hour later, Leena made five trips up and down the staircase, carrying gallon jars filled with sweet tea. Tabby had ten pizzas cut into thin slices. She ordered five cheese and five pepperoni. She also ordered three dozen chocolate chip cookies, halved and her friend donated paper plates and cups. The price was low enough for petty cash to cover it.

They set the spread on the table in the reading room and Leena's spirit perked up. People came in and browsed while chowing down on a piece of pizza. She snatched a cookie and took her place behind the counter at the cash register.

Thoughts of Roger filled her mind and made her smile, then she laughed when her cell phone buzzed and it was him.

"I was just thinking about you. How was your meeting?"

She paused, listening to him change the subject, and then answered, "I don't know, I can ask. Hang on.

"Tabby, I know we'd plans for a party today but Roger says he really needs me to go with him. It's another murder and he wants me with him. Can you handle the store without me, possibly for the whole day?"

"Yes, I can...no problem. This explains your restless night and mood."

Leena looked surprised at her statement and then, thought how perceptive the young girl was. They made a good pair.

"Go...tell him you'll go," Tabby insisted.

"Roger? Yeah, go ahead and pick me up. You're what?" She laughed when she looked out the window and saw him sitting in his car. "I'll be out in a minute."

As soon as she disconnected, she sent Bradly a text message which stated she had to reschedule. He texted back he understood.

Her purse was upstairs, so she ran one last time up to her apartment. She came back, thanked Tabby, and apologized in the same sentence. Roger stood by her car door, holding it open. Her hand brushed over his.

"You sounded serious."

"This one's pretty bad, Leena. The manner of death is the same, but he stepped it up a bit. He's taunting us openly now. Sit back and relax, we've about a thirty minute ride."

He took Conti Street up to Bourbon Street and over to Esplanade, where he caught Interstate Ten heading

Northeast. Silence filled the car. He didn't even turn on any music which she thought was odd for him. He always had music going. Slowing her breathing, she closed her eyes, and concentrated on calming her emotions. Once her body relaxed, she focused on her Tarot cards and what she'd learned from them over the years. True to her belief in them, it calmed her.

Once they were on Interstate Ten, the trip went faster. He exited at Bullard Avenue, making a right hand turn. From Bullard, he made a left onto Lake Forest Boulevard, which took him straight to the abandoned Six Flags over New Orleans.

"We're about two miles away now. Bryan said I'd be totally shocked at what I saw."

"Does he know you're bringing me? You know, he's got a problem with me and what I can do?"

"He knows. In fact, it was his idea. You've gained a partial believer."

"That surprises me a great deal." Sarcasm filled her voice.

She saw he'd flipped on his blinker, prepared to take the next exit. Off in the distance, skeletons of roller coaster rides and shells of buildings could be seen. An eerie feeling came over her, turning into extreme dread.

"This feels evil, Roger."

"It is, baby. Extremely evil."

He drove around old barricades at the front of the park, driving to the location where the investigating team parked their vehicles. The closer they got to the spot, the more of the devastation Katrina caused could be seen.

Leena was sickened by the destruction left behind. This had been a place of fun for kids and families. Now, it was simply sad. Her eyes scanned the parts of the park she could see from where they sat, until they saw the outline of the Ferris wheel. Halfway up on one side of the wheel, something large was hanging from the bottom of one of the carts.

"What in the hell is that?" she asked.

"It's a body. They're using a cherry picker to get her down, but they have to be careful to make sure they don't destroy evidence doing it."

"It's not tall enough for a human body."

"Bryan told me, her body was bent in a ball and tied up with rope. Leena, this murder was different. He let her bleed onto the ground. The blood wasn't collected. We won't know for sure about prints, until we get her down. Then the forensic team can go over her body. They'll have to go back up in the bucket in order to print the cart, but I doubt it will show anything.

"Oh, my God, Roger. Are you sure it's the same killer?"

"Yes, we are. He simply stepped up his game to the next level. Can you do this or do you need to wait in the car until I'm through?"

"Yeah, I can do this. Let's go and get this over with."

They strode together, neither one saying a word, seeming as if they were walking through a graveyard on their way to a funeral. The amusement park no longer had life and neither did the victim. It was spilled on the ground to mingle with the decay of the park. Not much of a fair ending for a woman to endure.

She and Roger stood near the cherry picker, observing one man carefully cutting the rope which held the body to the Ferris wheel. Another man, waited to catch the bundle to keep it from falling.

Once they had the body, they lowered the bucket to it normal position and handed the body over to the forensics team. Together, the two moved to the front of the truck, studying the scene. The girl was young, naked, and bound with thick rope, tied in ornamental knots. She perceived how her arms were crossed and tied together around her chest. The knees were bent to her chest, fastened with the ropes, and wound around her calves and feet. All wrapped up beautifully in a package of gorgeous knots.

Chapter Eighteen

Leena continued to stare at the body, mentally noting the position it was in.

"Roger, you remember I told you about my dream the other afternoon? This was the position I was frozen in by you. I didn't think anything about it because it was you, and I was simply immobile, not bleeding."

"Her wrists and neck were cut, with her body hung upside down to speed the blood loss."

"I don't understand the ropes. Why the flashy knotting?"

"It's called Shibari, an ancient Japanese form of rope bondage…another part of BDSM. Several Doms enjoy tying their subs to restrict movement and bring them to orgasm. I don't know much about it, except the subs seem to like it. They also love the different ways to be displayed and bound. It's quite beautiful."

"Not for murder, it's not," she snapped. She saw the color of the girl's skin, and turned away. Her face couldn't be seen and Leena was glad. Eyes which have lost life are frightening, she thought.

Across the park from behind the Ferris wheel, Bryan was hoofing it toward the two. His face looked determined to her and she spied a plastic bag in his hand.

"Hey Roger, what do you think?"

"It's pretty bad, Bry. You're right, I was definitely shocked."

"Hi Leena, thanks for coming. Can you make out anything from all this mess?"

"Not yet, Bryan. I won't be able to touch the body until forensics is through with her. I really don't think I need to ride up in the bucket and touch the wheel."

"I can see your point. You might be interested in this, though." He handed the evidence bag to her. Inside, was another Tarot card with her name etched on it. It was covered in blood. "I picked it off the ground when I first arrived on the scene. It was laying directly under the victim, I guess so the blood could drip on it. Since the body was high in the air, the blood didn't always drip straight down. There's a wide area of blood soaked cement and soil," Bryan explained.

She turned the bag over in her hands several times, studying the card.

"It's the Wheel of Fortune card. Usually, it's a good omen card but in this case, I don't think so. We consider it the destiny, fate, or karma card. Because it can bring luck into it, one must always think before they act. It can be a major turning point in a person's life. For this situation, I think he's telling me my fate or destiny is tied to him. Of course, I can't be totally certain without the influence of other cards surrounding the Wheel."

She handed the package back to Bryan. His eyes held hers for a moment and she thought he would say something. But he turned and paced over to the team, handing the bag off to them.

Everywhere she turned, deserted buildings and broken park rides glared back at her. She felt cold and alone, but most of all she felt threatened. A warm arm wound around her waist, drawing her close, made her feel secure.

"Come on. I'm taking you home. Not sure it was such a good idea to bring you with me."

"No, I'm glad you did. I needed to know."

As they went toward their car, Bryan caught up with them.

"They just got a hit on facial recognition. The woman was a twenty-five year old fortune teller from the

Lakeview area. She was single, living with two female roommates," he told them.

"How did you do that?" she asked.

"Smart phone. They took a close-up picture and ran it through the city's database."

"Thanks, Bryan, for the info. I'll talk with you tomorrow. Okay, little lady, what do you say we go home, grab a pizza, some beer, and watch a movie?"

She elbowed him in the ribs. "You remember what happened the last time we had pizza and beer?"

"I'm counting on it," he teased back.

"You're incorrigible, Sir."

"Also, we can plan our logistics pertaining to dinner with James tomorrow night. See, there's enough to keep us busy and not think about what happened here today."

"Oh yeah, I'd almost forgotten."

"You'll enjoy James. He's different than when he's at the club. A good friend and one hell of a poker player. Not sure I've ever known him to cook, though. It'll be interesting."

They drove back to her apartment, stopping for food on the way. The evening didn't quite end up as Roger planned. Leena was tired and before he knew it, she'd fallen asleep during the movie. He didn't have the heart to wake her, so he held her in his arms and let her sleep.

****

When Leena and Roger stepped down the stairs toward his Challenger, she couldn't get over how tired her mind and body were. Yesterday had disturbed her more than she'd been willing to admit. The killer's open challenge rattled her emotions.

She would've loved to have stayed in bed all day, but her guilt at leaving Tabby alone yesterday, prevented her from doing so. And oh, how she would love to skip out of this dinner tonight. No, she wouldn't cut out on Roger. She'll go and be the perfect dinner guest.

Once they arrived at the club, Roger escorted her into the elevator up to the third floor. They moved down the hall to another one at the opposite end. He punched in a numerical code, opening the doors. They rode it to the fourth floor, where the doors opened into the private quarters of Master James.

She'd never been in this part of the club before. Miss Lilly didn't give her the grand tour on the first night they visited. It was on the top floor, above the private apartments used for role playing. As Master James gave them a tour, she wasn't surprised at the décor of the living room. Dark hard wood floors, paneled walls with solid mirrors on one, and a brick wall where the two way fire place stood. The other side of the fireplace opened into his huge bedroom. His kitchen was large and totally stainless steel with marble counter tops. The shine alone, made her squint her eyes.

There were no windows and the ceiling was tall. She'd no idea there were so many floors in the building. The men were chatting back and forth about the operations of the club. Not paying attention to their conversation, she couldn't help but notice James' eyes were constantly on her. She wondered if Roger noticed. He had tremendous respect for the Master, and considered him a friend and great boss. She thought about how many times Master James had hit on her to play in the club, and wondered if Roger suspected.

Besides his bedroom, there was an office, three bathrooms, and two guest bedrooms. Leena was in awe of the apartment. Four of her apartments could fit inside his. At the end of the hallway, was another door he didn't approach.

"What's behind the last door, Master James? Do we get to see?"

"I'm sorry. This room is my own private playroom and is currently being renovated. It's also where I draw up plans for new equipment. Maybe you'll grace me as my own personal guinea pig one day?"

Her eyes shot to Roger's, begging him to help her get out of the situation. James was grinning at her as she shot him a go to hell look.

"I'm afraid I'd have to intervene and decline for Leena, James. At the moment, she's totally my submissive." She breathed a huge sigh of relief.

"Quite understandable, Roger. I wouldn't let anyone else touch her if she were mine. Shall we head back to the dining room for dinner? I'm sure the caterers have the food laid out by now."

"You didn't cook for us?" Leena teased.

"Truth be told, Sweet Girl, I'm a horrible cook. I've a housekeeper who cooks for me. She's quite wonderful in many ways."

The dinner was Italian with various kinds of pastas, sauces, meats, breads, and salads. The wine flowed abundantly which was a good thing. Even with Roger close beside her, she was uncomfortable around the head Master and owner of the club. If Roger noticed, he didn't react to it.

She preferred the Alfredo sauce instead of the marinara. Her mouth savored the creamy, thick mixture of sauce and pasta as she held it in her mouth, slowly chewing. A taste of pure heaven was what ran through her thoughts, when Roger's phone buzzed. Her eyes dropped, fear rising in her chest because in her heart, she knew another murder had been committed.

Roger excused himself from the table as she watched him stand and leave the room. She wanted to go with him, but knew it would be out of character for a submissive.

"May I refill your wine, my dear?"

"Yes, please. Thank you, Sir."

As he stood next to her, he leaned over her shoulder to pour the wine, practically touching her. He stood much too close for her liking.

"May I ask you a personal question, Sir?" She hoped she'd change his focus to something else, other than the close contact. Roger would definitely need to know about this.

"Of course, Child, anything."

"Why do you always wear those black leather gloves? I've seen you wear them at the club when you're doing a scene and when you're just watching. You're wearing them now."

His eyes sparkled as he smiled at her. "I've a skin condition where I must keep the skin protected from the light. Rather than take them off and on, several times a day, I simply choose to wear them at all times, except when I sleep."

"I'm sorry. I don't mean to pry…I was curious if it was a fashion thing or something else."

"You're fine…no harm done."

Roger barreled into the room, looking unhappy.

"I'm sorry, James, but we're going to have to cut this short. There's been another murder and they're insisting I come to the scene at once. Please forgive our having to rush off, but I need to take Leena home before I head to the crime scene. Can we have a rain check?"

"Of course, Roger, anytime. I hate the fact you both aren't going to be able to finish your dinner. Poor Leena's barely started her alfredo."

"I know. We'll make it up to you. I'm sorry, Leena, I know you're starved after today."

"It's fine…I've stuff at home I can fix. Let me get my purse."

"I tell you what," chimed in Master James. "Why don't you go ahead to your investigation and I'll box up some of this food for you both, and then take her home. Then, she can enjoy her meal with you later, you can do your job, and know she's safe and sound."

"I couldn't put you out like that," Roger stated.

"Nonsense…you're not putting me out. I'm delighted to help. I'm sure they probably needed you there thirty minutes ago. You don't mind do you, Leena? I promise I don't bite and I'll drive safely."

Her heart sank into her stomach, her mind screaming Hell No at Roger. But he smiled at her, as if he thought it was a great idea. She knew she couldn't blow their cover of Dom and sub, so she swallowed hard.

"No, it'd be very nice of you, Master James. If you're sure you don't mind? I could call a taxi."

"I wouldn't hear of it. I don't mind one bit. You go ahead, Roger, while we pack up here and head out. I hope it's not another psychic killing."

"You and me both, James." He sauntered over to Leena, took her in his arms, and placed a demanding kiss on her lips.

Leena's heart sank watching him get into the elevator, the doors closing in front of him. She told herself she was being silly and had nothing to worry about. Master James was Roger's friend and boss. Still, her intuition was screaming a warning in her brain. Her eyes focused on her food, as he walked into the dining room, from seeing Roger off. She started to stand and help him pack up the food.

"Please, sit. We've got plenty of time. Let me get you another glass of wine."

"I really need to go. I'm afraid I'll be tipsy before too long."

"I'll let you taste one of my favorite Bordeaux wines. It's a bit lighter than most so it shouldn't make you tipsy." She viewed him strolling to his wine cabinet and selecting a bottle from the shelf. He poured a small amount in a new wine glass for her.

"It really has a wonderful bouquet and flavor…subtly mellows you without all the buzzing."

Begrudgingly, she held the glass under her nose, swirling it, and finally took a sip. She hated to admit it, but it was excellent.

"It's very good, Master James. You've got excellent taste."

"I'd have to agree with you, Child. My tastes in various areas lean toward excellence and some would say, wicked extravagance."

Once her glass was empty, she sat back in her chair feeling more comfortable with the situation. She genuinely smiled at the Dom without any misgivings what-so-ever.

"You look beautiful, my dear. Your hair, skin color, and those remarkable eyes are gorgeous. You mentioned my locked room earlier, would you like to see inside? I'm working on a new toy for the club."

"You'd really show it to me? I'd love to see it, Sir. I'd be honored."

"And so you shall, my sweet, so you shall."

When she stood, a wave of dizziness hit her head. Staggering slightly, she grabbed the back of her chair for support.

"I'm afraid the wine wasn't as light as you thought, Sir. I'm definitely a little bit tipsy."

"Not a problem. Here, simply lean on me and thread your arm through mine. I'll get you safely down the hall."

"It's awfully nice of you, Sir. Thank you." For some crazy reason, she was feeling a bit giddy and very trusting of him. They joked and laughed while making their way to the locked door.

Her body dragged a bit but she wasn't worried, since he navigated her perfectly to the room. There was a keypad on the wall and she tried to focus on the set of numbers he punched in. She heard a buzz, and then the door popped open.

It opened into a large, plush room with velvet wall coverings the color of her emerald green eyes. Her vision slowly blurred while staring at a huge, silver Z sitting in the middle of the room. She leaned further into his arms.

Her words slurred. "I'm not feeling so hot, Sir. I need to go home now."

The last thing she heard was, "No worries…I've got you."

Chapter Nineteen

Leena's arms ached, her eyes blurred, and her head hurt. She tried to stretch, but couldn't move. The more she attempted to move, the more frustration and confusion took over. She realized finally, her eyes were covered and had no idea where she was or what was wrong with her.

Think Leena. What was the last thing you remember?

Moans...she heard moaning. Finally, she discovered they were coming from her.

Oh, shit. I'm in trouble.

"It looks like our girl is coming around, James. It's about time. How much did you give her for Christ's sake?"

"Not enough to put her out this long. Her tolerance level must be low," he answered.

Leena could hear voices mumbling in the distance. Try as she might, she couldn't understand what was being said or recognize any of them. She did understand one was male and one female, but nothing else.

She wished she could move around to clear her head, but it was impossible. Whatever was holding her down, was strong. Suddenly, hands slapped her face, on one side and then the other. It hurt like hell…they weren't soft pats. If she could reach up and grab those hands, she'd make them stop. Anger flooded through her as the slapping continued, spurring her adrenalin into overdrive. Low and guttural, a growl built deep in her throat, until she finally shouted.

"Stop hitting me!"

"I think our guest of honor is finally awake," the female taunted. The woman's fingers stroked softly over Leena's breast and then pinched the crap out of it.

"Ow! That hurts!"

"It was meant to, Child. We need you alert as well as awake," the woman snarled.

She recognized the voice then. No one else but Lilly called her Child. No, wait, so did James.

"Lilly, is that you? What have you done to me? Why are you doing this?"

The blindfold was jerked off her face, letting the light hit her eyes. She tried to focus, but it wasn't happening fast enough. Her eyes closed as she dropped her head against whatever she'd been tied to.

"Give it time, you'll understand soon enough. All your questions will be answered once your vision and head has cleared," the voice belonging to James told her. She knew it was James, because Lilly used his name.

Whatever her body was attached to, Leena felt it tilt up into an upright position, but wasn't standing on her feet.

Her body was actually attached to the equipment. Once her body was in a stable position, she opened her eyes and focused on her tormentors. James was directly in front of her, with Lilly standing on his left side. And in the back, much to her surprise, and watching hungrily, was Paul.

Oh God, they're all in on this?

"What's going on guys?"

James spoke up. "You're our fortune teller for the evening, Leena. I'm especially excited about having you, because of your special talent. I can taste the energy all ready."

"Haven't you figured this out yet, Child? And Addie said you were so smart and gifted." Lilly hatefully sneered at her. Paul stayed in the background, his eyes gleaming. It made her shiver.

Tears pooled in her eyes, looking from one face to the other. "Lilly, you're the shock here. I never thought once you were my enemy. Did you help kill Nana? Why?"

"Oh look, she has true tears. Poor Leena. Addie was in my way. I was losing clients to her and the only reason I hung around was I thought she would leave the shop to me. Imagine my surprise when everything was left to you. So, I became your friend in order to stay close and learn, until Roger got in my way. Once he wouldn't let you investigate with anyone but himself, I had to bow out."

By this time, the tears were streaming down her face. "My aunt loved you. She considered you her best friend and family. How could you have hated her so much?"

"Simply because Addie was gifted, like you. Her readings were always accurate and I got sick of hearing her clients brag about her. It was hard enough for me to pick information from my clients in order to give them a believable reading. When a few of mine went to Addie and her predictions came true, I'd had enough of Miss Addie Price."

"You helped kill her?"

"No Child, I only told James where she'd be and suggested he do a fortune teller theme killing spree. We've been friends for a very long time. I was aware of his unusual tastes but I accepted him anyway. It was a beautiful plan."

"Unusual tastes? I don't understand. What does being a Master have to do with draining your victims dry?"

"I think this is where I take center stage, beautiful. I assume you know about Vampires?" James chimed in.

"Yes, I know what they are, but they don't really exist," Leena shot back.

"Oh, but they do, my dear. I'm living proof of it. We're called human vampires and we need blood the same as our fictional counterparts do. Twenty-five years ago, I was diagnosed with a severe form of porphyria. It's a genetic abnormality of the hemoglobin part of the blood. It explained the total lack of energy I experienced as well as an extreme sensitivity to light. I researched everything I could about the illness and when a report came out years later stating human vampirism was in no way related to porphyria, I moved here. New Orleans is noted for their groups of human vampires. At first, I thought the local covens and associations would be helpful to me, but there were too many rules to follow. I struck out on my own and searched for people who'd willingly donate their blood to me. The energy I gained from drinking their blood, helped tremendously for a while. Sadly, like everything else, it took more and more blood to keep my level up. People in the community labelled me crazy and dangerous. They refused to let me take more of their blood. So taking matters into my own hands, I took the homeless from the street, fed them, and built their strength up. Then, I drained them, disposed of the bodies in the bayous, and drank my fill, storing the rest. Unfortunately, sometimes it took quite a bit longer to build their bodies up to the point I wanted. Their blood didn't work on me as well as it once did."

Nausea filled her stomach as she listened to his cavalier words and tone. She realized how horrible her situation was. Barely seeing through her tears, she saw Paul standing in the back, observing her the way a hungry lioness views her prey. His eyes roamed over her naked body.

"I want to do her now, Master James. Let me taste her pussy before I shove my cock into her."

"Paul, no one is going to *do* her. She's pristine and I want her to stay that way."

Leena's eyes caught Lilly giving Master James a dirty look, which he seemed to ignore.

"She's a treasure to be savored and cherished. Her gift will energize me beyond my wildest dreams. We'll torture her...build panic in her, so her psychic power will become active. But I won't have her spoiled like a common fortune teller."

"All right," Lilly butted in. "Let's get on with this. We're wasting time. I want her dead and out of the way. It's going to take forever to get rid of all the evidence in this room. It was a stupid idea to do it here to begin with. I for one, don't intend to spend the whole night cleaning up."

Leena listened to them argue with each other, wondering how they could even work together. It was obvious to her, they didn't like each other. Master James had already laid out a procedure tray with various items on it.

"Shall we start, my dear? Did you notice you were attached to my newest invention? Rather than a St. Andrews cross, I've developed a universal bondage table in the shape of a Z. It's stainless steel, easy to clean, and motorized to stand you up or lay you down. Right now, I'm laying you down in order to attach several items onto your body. Once your emotions are out of control, your eyes will tell me when it's time to harvest your blood. Here we go."

The table started to lower and she struggled hopelessly to get free of the restraints. "You're crazy, James. You're all crazy," she shouted.

"Several of the human vampire groups told me the same thing, years ago. I'm not crazy, I'm surviving. You should feel honored to be a part of it."

"Please don't do this," she begged.

"No use begging, dear, it really doesn't suit you. Paul, come put the nipple clamps on her breasts."

His eyes twinkled with pleasure as she watched him walk to the tray, picking up two adjustable nipple clamps. He grabbed her right breast, roughly squeezing it, then painfully pinching it while grinning at her. Attaching the clamp over her nipple, he turned the knob, tightening it past her comfort level.

By the time the second clamp was placed, she cried and screamed. He went back for a third clamp and attached it to her clit in the same manner. Her pain threshold had been surpassed with the second clamp but this one threw her over the edge. Her screams were constant now, begging them to stop the pain. She tried hard to calm herself but the pain was so intense, she couldn't get it under control.

A sharp burning flew across her mound and then her thighs, at the same time a loud smack was heard. She looked up and Lilly was smiling with a cane in her hands.

"Keep your eyes open, love. Master James needs to be able to see when your power has kicked in."

The woman caned her again across both areas. She then hit her five more times.

The girl's crying grew louder, screaming for the woman to stop. The woman, however, was relentless. Taking her time, she hit Leena ten more times in the very same spots. Master James finally stepped in, halting Lilly's action.

"Look into my eyes, my dear, so I can see where we are. Hmm, close but not quite there. Lilly continue."

With each of the next twenty strikes, Leena could feel herself sinking into the middle of her pain, hoping to die. After the twentieth blow, the Dom stopped the older woman once more.

"Leena, open your eyes for me, Sweet Girl. Let me see."

She barely opened her eyes, letting the tears spill down her cheeks.

"Breathtaking. Look at those beautiful emerald green eyes. I could get lost in them. Now it's my turn. Lilly, stand by her hips. Paul, go around on the other side opposite me. Right there. Now, when I reach three, I want you two to take the clamp off her body at the same time I remove mine. You'll have to loosen it a little but only ease the clamp enough to be able to yank it off. One...two...three...now."

The young girl had never felt such pain in her life. She didn't know it could get any worse than before, but it did. She vomited what little of her dinner there was, and Master James had to raise the table in order for her not to choke.

****

Roger was pissed they'd called him in. It wasn't the serial killer even though they worked it up as if it were. He knew this because of several things. There was no BDSM influence involved at all…no bondage, no tables or toys. The murder scene was sloppy…not clear of evidence like the others. The CSI's found blood spilled everywhere, taking samples to do a comparison between them. Fingerprints were abundant, as if they were deliberately placed in plain sight. But the most important aspect was the fact the woman didn't appear to be a fortune teller. Her purse was found with her ID inside. She had a business card for an out of town insurance agency. The name and picture matched the driver's license.

"Okay guys, who told you to bring me down here?"

One young police officer gulped and answered. "I did, Sir. I thought it was a clear case of the psychic killer."

"And what gave you that impression? Have you worked on the other crime scenes? Did you spend hours upon hours profiling this perp?"

"No, Sir."

"Next time, wait for the coroner before you announce your thoughts as facts."

"Yes, Sir."

He took his cell phone out of his pocket and punched in Leena's number. It went straight to voice mail, confusing him. Maybe he misdialed, he thought, and punched the number again only slower. Again it immediately went to voice mail, and it set off all his alarms. He knew she should be at her apartment by now, waiting on him. He punched in Bryan's number, waiting for him to answer.

"Hey Roger. Was it another psychic murder?"

"No, it looks like a copycat to me. Are you still parked outside of the club with your eyes on Leena?"

"Yeah, I'm here but she hasn't come out yet. I thought you said James was driving her home. Maybe she decided to spend the night and play."

"Knock it off, Bryan. I'm not in the mood for your cracks about her. Leena wouldn't play…something's very wrong. She's not answering her phone. Can you find a way to get into the club and go up to the fourth floor? Master James' apartment is up there. There's a dedicated elevator at the end of the hall on the third floor. The elevator opens directly into the living room, so be careful. I'm calling this in for backup, then I'll head your way."

"Roger, if you're wrong, you'll face disciplinary action with the Captain."

"I don't care, Bryan. I'm not wrong…I know it."

"Okay, get your ass over here quick. I don't like going in without my partner having my back."

"Love you too, Moron."

Roger disconnected from his partner and called the station for backup.

"Yeah, this is detective Roger Black, badge number D77. I need all units near The Secret Whispers Club on Rampart Street just off Toulouse, for backup for a possible murder. Detective Bryan Hall is already on the scene. I'm on the way there as soon as I hang up."

Chapter Twenty

Hands were slapping Leena's face again. Compared to the pain from her lower body, the slaps were nothing. She wanted to ignore them, but the hands hit harder and harder. She finally opened her eyes, focusing through blurry vision at Master James smiling face.

"There you are, my dear. I was afraid we'd lost you. You must be awake while I finish. You'll be my crowning glory."

Tired, and only wanting to sleep, but she knew they'd never let her.

"We'll do this slowly so your energy isn't depleted all at once. We don't need to rush here."

Her eyes traveled to his face, wondering how he thought he could go slowly. Roger was probably already aware she hadn't been taken home. Unless of course, if he wasn't swamped with the current murder. Her heart sank.

She looked at his hands, noticing the gloves were now gone. He grabbed her right wrist and immediately, her body jolted as she saw visions of all three murders. His smiling face looked down at each victim the way he looked at her. Reality came back when her wrists burned like fire. He held a scalpel in his hands after slicing across her arm.

Her loud screams rose to a high pitch, as he placed her hand and wrist in a clear, vinyl bag. He then sealed the bag to her arms with surgical tape. Slowly, blood trickled down her hand, dripping into the bag.

"My God, can she not stop incessantly screaming?" complained Lilly. "Let me just gag her James, please?"

Leena watched him frown at the woman, as he moved to the left side of the table.

"You're not to touch this girl, Lilly. You played your part and I won't allow you to do any more."

Pain burned through her left wrist as he sliced across it. It was bagged in the same manner. The table moved slowly to the upright position again, to let gravity take its course with the bleeding. Once in place and stopped, her eyes were staring directly into his. She could feel his breath blowing across her face.

"Such a beautiful, vibrant young woman. A shame we never got to play. I think you would've enjoyed it."

"I doubt it," she whispered.

His fingers stroked the skin on her throat up and down. He placed them on her artery, seeming to be pleased with the pulsing of her heart.

"Strong heart as well as soft skin. Your strength will be put to good use, Child."

Her eyes caught him staring at the wall behind her and thought she saw panic fill his eyes. In seconds, he turned and shouted.

"Paul, the light's on…someone's in the elevator. Check it out."

It was difficult for her to stay alert and coherent. Her mind wanted to give up. It was too late for anyone to help her now, James had already started bleeding her. At least it's what she told herself.

"Lilly, bring me a fresh surgical kit from the shelf behind you. Oh, and also one of the large EDTA bags with the tubing attached."

Lilly snapped at him. "I'm not your servant, James. Why do you need a fresh kit? Just use the scalpel you have on your tray."

"Obviously, you don't understand hygiene versus bacterial infection. I've no intention of introducing something into her blood which can infect me. Hopefully, you take better care of your whores."

Lilly threw the kit and bag on the tray, stomped over to a chair, and plopped in it.

"Impossible bitch. I've no idea why I even bother with you anymore."

"Because you need me to find the good psychics, that's why," she snarled.

He directed his attention back to the young girl. "Okay, Baby Girl, I'm going to start prepping your throat now. Soon it'll be all over, you'll grow tired, and fall into a deep sleep."

Leena's brain was foggy as she tried to watch him while he took four by four mesh squares soaked in surgical soap, and cleaned her neck on both sides. She gave up trying to see him, closed her eyes, not wanting to watch or deal with him any longer.

Thoughts of Roger filled her mind. Oh, how she wanted to be in his bed, in his arms. She'd fought falling in love with him, always pushing him away. He'd been persistent and she was grateful for it. The past few weeks with him had been thrilling and fun. She'd never had sex where she could feel the pure love of the person with her. With Roger, she knew he loved her.

I wish I could tell you what you mean to me, how you make me feel loved. I'm sorry I never said the words. I love you, Roger. God, how I love you.

James' voice roused her from her dream.

"Lilly, wake up you stupid woman. How long has Paul been gone?"

Burning…Leena's neck was burning on the right side. "Hurts," she barely whispered before falling asleep again.

"Lilly, look at the clock! How long has Paul been gone? I'm inserting the cannula and I can't turn and look."

"All right, give me time. He's been gone thirty minutes. He probably got lost in your apartment."

"Go look for him. Something's not right. He's been in my apartment before."

"I'm not going out there. You do your own dirty work."

"You'll go or I'll change my blood preference to Ladies of the Evening and I'll start with yours."

****

Roger reached Secret Whispers just as a few backup vehicles pulled up. He ran ahead of them, leading the way. Truth was, he had to get to Leena. Bryan had called him after he'd taken some young guy out, who tried to jump him. He'd checked the entire apartment but found no one else but the punk.

Roger knew where they were. They were in the locked room James had been reluctant to show them. He'd bust down the door if he had to. It'd been forty-five minutes since he'd left the murder…much too long for it to be good for her. The killer had to be James…no other explanation. He'd never forgive himself for leaving her with him.

If he hurt her, I'll kill him.

When he reached the apartment, he found Bryan in the kitchen with the kid cuffed and lying face down.

"Is he alive, Bry?"

"Yeah, I just rang his bell once or twice. I can wake him up."

"Good, get started then. We need him for the code to the keypad lock on the door at the end of the hall. And we need surprise to be on our side. Get the bastard up and don't let him give you no for an answer."

He watched Bryan take ice, put it into a pitcher, and filled it with water, stirring it. Roger rolled the guy over and took a step back. "Well, look who we have here. Hello Paul."

His partner slowly poured the ice cold water into Paul's face. Coughing and sputtering, Paul cussed as well as threatened the two detectives. When he looked around and saw the number of police officers standing at the side, he calmed down.

"Now, we have your attention, I want the code to the keypad of the room," ordered Roger.

"I don't know what you're talking about. I don't have any code."

Roger averted his eyes when he saw Bryan kick the young man in the ribs. Then he jerked him up by the collar.

"Do you remember the code now or do I need to kick your other ribs too?"

Roger held his hand up, stopping Bryan. He pulled out his revolver, placing it in Paul's mouth.

"If you don't give me the code, I'll pull the trigger, and splatter your brain all over Master James' kitchen. Now give me the damn code!"

He pulled back the hammer, and stared hard into Paul's eyes. The perp shook his head up and down, the best he could, and Roger slowly pulled the gun from his mouth.

"It's the street address of the club plus the current month and year."

Roger stepped back from him and turned to the other officers in the room.

"He's all yours…don't be gentle with him. Bryan and I will need a few of you to come with us. I don't know what we're going to find in the room."

"Oh, and send the paramedics up to the door and tell them to wait until I yell for them. I'm afraid of how much blood won't be left in Leena. They'll need to help her once we get James under control."

Four officers took Paul down the elevator and outside to the squad car. The rest followed behind the detectives. When Roger reached the door, his hands were shaking. His adrenalin surged through his body, making it difficult to punch in the code, as well as hold on to his gun.

Just when he focused on entering the numbers, the door swung open with Lilly standing in shock, wide eyed.

"Shit!" she shouted as she tried to slam the door in their faces.

He and Bryan had stood ready to rush the door once it was unlocked. They hit the door with enough force, it knocked Lilly back into the room on her ass. Bryan and two officers pinned her down and cuffed her. She tried to fight them off, but the three of them were too strong.

"Get your fucking hands off me! I've done nothing wrong."

"Shut up, Bitch," growled Bryan, slapping handcuffs on her. "Take her out of here. Make sure the paramedics know where this room is."

Roger was a statue, glaring at James, pointing his gun at his friend, who was holding a scalpel to Leena's throat. His eyes briefly surveyed the bags, noting how much blood had pooled at the bottom of all three. She wasn't conscious.

"What're you doing, James? Put down the scalpel and let's talk."

"I'm afraid I need your woman's blood, Roger, and I'm taking it."

"Just take the blade away from her throat. We can work through this. You don't need to do this."

"But I do...you see, she's so special. Her gifts are real and her blood will restore my strength far better than anyone else."

"I don't understand, my friend. How is that going to happen?"

"I'm a human vampire, my boy. I need blood to keep my body whole and strong. I drink blood and I'm going to drink hers. Put your gun away and leave, or I swear, I'll slit her throat. She'll bleed out faster than she already is."

"I can't do what you ask. Whether I lower my weapon or not, you'll cut her anyway. Please, put the blade down."

"I'm sorry, Roger, I truly am. I know you love her very much but this is my life I'm fighting for." In a matter of seconds, he'd run the blade across her neck. The next few moments, Roger saw it in slow motion…the cut, the line of blood, the bullet flying out of the nose of his gun, heading for James' head, who'd already sunk his mouth onto her throat.

The bullet exploded the back of James' head after he'd taken his first and only drink of Leena. He fell to the floor, tangled in the tubing, and pulling it out of her neck. Blood was squirting everywhere.

Roger and Bryan both ran to her, applying pressure to the cut.

"Get the paramedics in here now!" Roger shouted. "Leena, stay with me. You damn well better stay with me."

"Her pulse is weak, Roger. I can barely feel one on this side."

"Where the hell are those paramedics?" Roger shouted once again, as two paramedics ran into the room, taking over for the detectives. They immediately worked on closing the cut on her neck, and then took care of each wrist, releasing them from the bags. Two more brought a gurney into the room to transport her to the hospital. Once the wounds were stabilized, an IV was started and then they placed her on the gurney, wheeling her through the apartment, into the elevator. Roger followed on their heels.

"Hey man, I'll meet you at the hospital after I finish taking evidence. I'll wait on the crime scene investigators and fill them in," Bryan informed him.

"Thanks, Bryan. I appreciate it." He slapped him on the back, hugging him.

Epilogue

Three months later, Roger sat with Leena on a bench, watching the barges float up and down the Mississippi. He thought back on past events and gave thanks for the strength and fight in the woman beside him.

He rode in the ambulance with her, afraid she'd die before the ambulance arrived at the hospital. In the emergency room they drew blood for a type and cross match, immediately rushing it to the lab for testing. The doctor began stitching the cut across the jugular, before working on the others on her neck and wrists.

Within thirty minutes, he saw a nurse rush in and hang a unit of blood on her IV machine. A sigh of relief filled the air, when he saw the dark fluid flowing down the tubing into her arm. Until then, he'd stood at the back of the room, observing everything they did to her. He finally relaxed and sat in a chair by the door, trusting they'd take care of her.

When they first came into the ER, the doctors and nurses argued when he refused to leave Leena's side. Knowing his profession and the circumstances, they put him in the back and ignored him.

Another unit of blood was brought in and hooked up. Fatigue attacked Roger, almost knocking him to his knees, if he'd been standing. Even with being exhausted, he had no intention of going home.

When the doctor finished, he ordered her to be admitted and taken to ICU. On his way out the door, he stopped to talk with the young detective.

"You're Detective Black?"

"I am. How is she?"

"Thirty minutes later, and we wouldn't be having this conversation. She wouldn't be with us. We have her heavily sedated, to keep her quiet. She's lost a lot of blood. We're giving her two more units of blood and see where her levels are tomorrow morning. If they've improved significantly, we'll lower her sedation medication. I know I'll be talking to the wall when I tell you to go home and get some rest. Hopefully, tomorrow we'll know more about her prognosis."

Leena was in ICU for twenty-four hours and another seven days on a regular floor in the hospital. He never left her side, except when Bryan would stay with her while Roger went home to shower and change clothes.

Four days after her ordeal, Leena opened her eyes. He made sure his face was the first thing she saw. She blinked a few times, smiled, and whispered hoarsely, "Hi."

"Hello beautiful. It's so wonderful to see your eyes and smile. I was afraid I'd lost you. Please forgive me for leaving you alone with that monster. I didn't know."

"Shh…don't apologize. Not your fault. No one knew. You're here and it's all I care about," she croaked.

She touched his hand and he grabbed it with both of his, kissing her knuckles.

****

"You look like your mind is a million miles away," she said, pulling him back to reality.

"Not that far, Sweetness. I was remembering the night and weeks after."

"Why? It's over…in the past."

"I know. I remembered what you went through and how strong you were. I've never been more proud of you. You're a fighter, Leena."

"I had help. The hospital staff said you never left. After I was released, Tabby and you took care of me. If it hadn't been for the two of you, I'd have given up."

"Well, I don't think the Universe or your Nana would've let you get away with it."

She laughed but knew he was right. The Wheel of Fortune card hadn't been simply warning her. It also told her she'd overcome the trial and destiny would be on her side.

"So, now your wounds have healed, what have you decided to do?"

"My wounds have healed?" she laughed.

"The redness will fade, I promise."

"I intend to have tattoos placed around them. The one on my neck will be a permanent necklace. I'll be sexy…just wait and see."

"You're staying in New Orleans?"

"Why wouldn't I? I own my own business, I have an apartment, and great friends. Where else could I have all of those?"

"You just made my day, Sweetness. You'll be able to help me out every once in a while with your special talents."

"Oh, my, Roger, you do know how to sway a girl's mind."

"Think about how well we worked together. We're a perfect team. Bryan thinks so too."

"Then that settles it. After all, he has the final word."

Roger laughed and winked at her. She joined him in the laughter, loving the sound of it. Her mind traveled back to just before she passed out. She loved him and finally came to grips with it. The fear which James made her feel, at least made her face the truth. Not quite ready to tell him, though, but she knew it was coming.

"What'll happen to the club now?" she asked.

"The in-house Doms are meeting to vote on a new manager. It seems Master James owed a tremendous amount of money on the BDSM furniture and building. Several of the men are quite wealthy and will incorporate the place. It will still be in business only under new management."

"I'm not sure I could ever go back there. The pain he caused is still with me."

"I understand, baby. I'd never ask you to. Did I tell you, someone from RVOUS came to the hospital while you were unconscious?"

"What's RVOUS?"

"The Real Vampires of the United States. They represent a portion of the real vampire community in New

Orleans, but they have associations all over the states. He wanted you to know James was in no way affiliated with the real vampire community. Each house has rules and conduct regulations they follow. James had contacted them, but they realized not long after talking with him, the man was completely nuts. They don't normally share or let the outside communities know where they are, but he felt compelled to give you the information. He hoped you wouldn't think of real vampires as lunatics or murderers. To look at him, you'd never have known. He even brought flowers. He's quite cool."

Tears pooled in her eyes and she kissed him.

"You remember I told you we needed to go back to the Jackson Brewery Bistro Bar and eat there? Well, I made reservations, and we need to start that way."

They were seated in the back where they had a small amount of privacy and could hear. He ordered champagne and an appetizer.

"Are we celebrating something, Roger?" Fear gripped her, worrying he'd ask her a question she wasn't prepared to answer.

"Yes, we are." The waiter came with the bottle and poured the bubbly wine into their flutes. "We're celebrating life, friendship based on love, and the start of a magnificent partnership."

She clinked her glass against his and took a drink. The taste was wonderful, so she took another.

"This is delicious. I love champagne."

"I want you to know, Lena, how special you are to me. It would've destroyed me if things had turned out any different. I'll not rush you, or force you into a relationship you don't want. However, I think you're aware of my feelings. I look forward to growing our friendship and partnership. I look forward to sharing life together."

She thought for a moment and then added, "Here's to a fantastic partnership of crime solving, fortune telling, getting to know one another, and a life of love. Thank you, Roger, for all of it."

"Shall we order pizza and beer?" he asked.

"Trust me. You won't need them tonight," and she winked at him.

The End

About the Author

BIO of AJ Storm

A.J. Storm is an avid reader of BDSM, erotic paranormal romance, and lover of vampire and werewolf books. She currently lives in the Midwestern part of the United States with her husband of 39 years. She plays twelve string guitar and wrote love songs for her husband when they were dating. She loves all animals domesticated and wild. Extremely passionate about wolves and their habitat, the number one item on her Bucket List is to be able to physically interact with a wolf face to fur.

Her love of reading encouraged her to write her own daydreams down on paper and develop them into stories. When not reading, writing, or taking care of her husband, she spends time with her six grandchildren and two grown children.

AJ has previously published four books with Bitten Press LLC. The first was Emily's Passion. It was written to encourage women of a certain age to discover and believe desire and sexuality are still viable traits to their make-up. It also touches on breast cancer and the effects it can have on a woman and her frame of mind. These traits are still available to the mature woman and breast cancer survivor and Emily's Passion proves it.

Dark Strangers was AJ's second book. It deals with the age old war between vampires and werewolves. AJ jumps right in the middle of the dilemma striving to close the gap between the two species. Two sexy alphas, who are best friends, lead the way into uncharted territory...one a female vampire and the other a male wolf shifter. True love finds them in the midst of chaos, deception, and evil.

Alexander's Story is the second book in the Dark Strangers Trilogy and continues the saga of two paranormal species. This book delves into the cause of the rift between them and uses her hero to bring about the change needed. Of course, nothing is ever easy and evil has a way of staying one step ahead of good. Alexander's Story not only provides a means to an end, but new beginnings. Our hero finds HOT sex and true love in the process.

AJ's final book of the trilogy, The Power of Two, wraps up the story of our two families completing their goals, heartaches, and successes through generations to come.

An erotic murder mystery, set in the heart of New Orleans, will be released October 1, 2015. Fortune's Eyes is the story of a young woman who seeks sanctuary in the home of her aunt, but is immersed in the darker side of NOLA. Friended by a sexy homicide detective, they search the city for the serial killer targeting fortune tellers.

Made in the USA
Charleston, SC
14 November 2015